AYSHA JONAS

The Mother Diamond

A Fraidy Cat and Smarty Pants Adventure

AJ
BOOKS

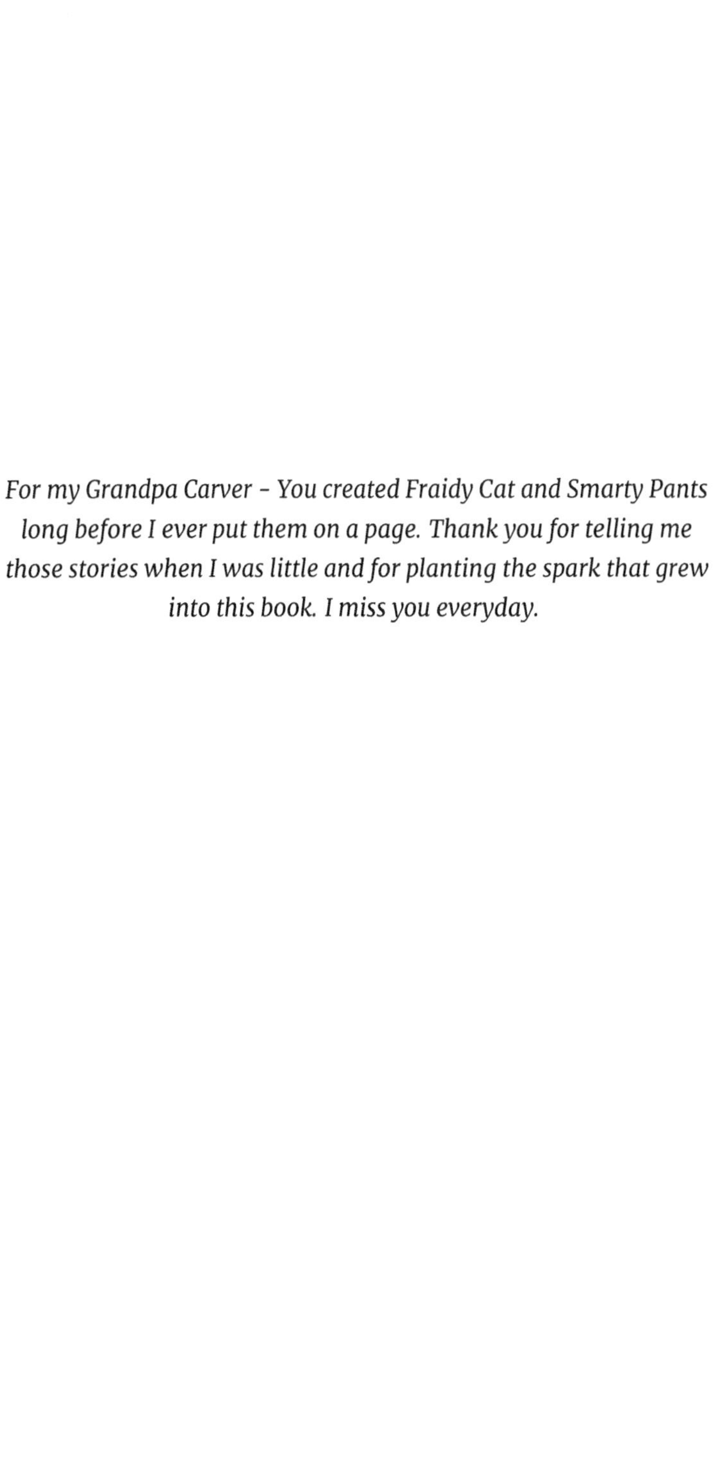

For my Grandpa Carver – You created Fraidy Cat and Smarty Pants long before I ever put them on a page. Thank you for telling me those stories when I was little and for planting the spark that grew into this book. I miss you everyday.

Contents

1

The Hidden Note

The cool summer breeze brushed the crumpled paper in Freddy's trembling hands. He sat hunched on his front porch steps, worry embedded across his face. The words on the note continually blurred and returned to focus as his amber brown eyes stared at the letter, barely noticing the crunch of footsteps on the gravel path leading up to his house.

"Fraidy!"

This shout could be heard from neighbors a block away, but Freddy, lost in thought, didn't look up.

"Fraidy Cat!"

Everyone called Freddy "Fraidy Cat", a nickname that stuck back in kindergarten because he'd jump at his own shadow and was too scared to enter the classroom without his mom holding his hand. As he got older, if called upon, he would freeze whenever he had to speak in class. Freddy was shy and kept to himself. He didn't go out of his way to make idle conversation with his peers. This only increased the use of them calling him this nickname, he was too scared to even talk to the kids he grew up with!

He used to hate the taunting name, until his best friend James told him to own it instead of letting it hurt him. He warned him that no one can have control over him, so don't give them that power.

Since that day, Freddy has worn the name like armor. And James, known around school as Smarty Pants, was always by his side. Together, Fraidy Cat and Smarty Pants were an inseparable team.

"Fraidy!" Smarty Pants called again, louder this time. When Fraidy Cat still didn't respond, Smarty Pants frowned, marched up the porch steps, and tugged the note right out of his friend's hands.

"Hey!" Fraidy blinked, startled, his sweaty hands now empty.

Smarty Pants turned the paper around and started reading before Fraidy could stop him.

Freddy,

I had to go. I don't know when I'll be back. Go to James' house if you need anything. If you get hungry, I made a sandwich for you in the fridge.

Love, Mom

Smarty Pants looked up from the letter, confused. "Where'd your mom go?"

Fraidy's mouth opened, but no words came out. His heart felt empty. He wondered the same thing. How could she leave him alone with just a note? He woke up from sleeping in and found the house empty. This was usual for summer, because mom would be at work showing a house to some buyers, but it was a Saturday and she had no showings on her schedule. She should have been home. She had never done anything like this before and Fraidy Cat didn't know how to react.

Seeing his friend frozen in place with worry, Smarty Pants sighed and guided him inside. "Come on," he said gently. "Let's get that sandwich she left for you."

The house was usually quiet since it was just Fraidy Cat and his mom who lived there. When Fraidy Cat was six years old, his dad, a firefighter, passed away on the job. With him gone, it was just Fraidy Cat and his mom, but with her missing, the house was too quiet. In this eerie silence, the smell of potato chips and lemon soap were more pronounced. They walked past the living room, which usually felt welcoming but now had a feeling of loneliness.

As they approached the kitchen, a variety of chairs decorated a large round table. Though only two people occupied the house, Smarty Pants' family, the Shelleys, were often invited for dinner and game night. Smarty Pants pulled out a chair from the table, the one with black trimming that Fraidy usually preferred. After waiting a moment for his friend to take a seat, he forcefully sat him down, still not waking him from his shock.

Smarty Pants made his way over to the refrigerator. It was adorned in school information papers, photos of happy memories, and a dry erase calendar that kept the family organized. He opened the fridge and spotted a plate wrapped in cling film. A yellow note was taped on top: Love, Mom.

He set the plate and a glass of cold water on the kitchen table in front of his friend. When Fraidy still didn't move, Smarty sat down beside him and started peeling off the cling film himself. The plastic crinkled loudly in the silence.

In the process of removing the cling film, the top slice of bread slid off the sandwich. Smarty Pants reached to fix it and paused. Something white peeked out from under the lettuce.

He lifted the lettuce leaf carefully. A folded piece of paper lay hidden beneath it.

"Fraidy," Smarty whispered, his curiosity sparking.

Fraidy's eyes widened. He snatched up the note, heart thudding. His mother's handwriting danced across the page, smudged, like she'd written it in a rush. He raced to open it, hoping the answer would lie inside but that couldn't have been further from the truth.

"It's a riddle," Fraidy murmured. His anxiety and worry about his mom were bubbling over, he wanted answers but he kept getting more questions.

Smarty leaned closer, reading over his shoulder. Dread was felt between both boys, but another feeling was lying dormant inside of Smarty. A feeling of intrigue and excitement over the mystery.

"We're going to solve it." He seized the mysterious note from his friend's hands and stood at the edge of the table. Like giving a presentation to his class, he recited the message from the note, hoping that an answer would appear on the dent-filled table. "To find the way, look beneath the light where shadows play," he read.

Before either of them could say another word, a forceful knock echoed from the front door. Both boys froze.

Another knock.

Then a voice: "Freddy? You in there? It's me. Mr. Kadburgler."

Fraidy exhaled in relief. "It's just my neighbor."

They shuffled to the living room, too many emotions running through their bodies to fully process what was happening. Fraidy Cat lifted the curtains to peer through the window beside the door, dust escaping into the fading sunlight. Mr. Kadburgler stood outside, waving politely. Fraidy opened the door and stepped aside, welcoming his neighbor in.

Mr. Kadburgler had always been a friendly but reclusive neighbor. He lived directly next to Fraidy Cat for the past few years and had only visited a handful of times. Even when outside watering his award winning petunias, he always wore a button up shirt, typically patterned with polka dots, that was buttoned up all the way to the top. He had a long mustache, speckled with gray hairs, that he had trained to curl up in two small circles that bounced every time he talked. He had always been polite to Fraidy Cat, but never showed a personality more than that.

Mr. Kadburgler welcomed himself into the living room. Following his lead, the boys also moved to take a seat in the living room, uncomfortable with the awkward encounter. Fraidy Cat and Smarty Pants sat next to each other on one couch. On the opposite side of the coffee table that held memories of playing card games, sat Mr. Kadburgler in his polka dotted button up.

"Hello, boys," said Mr. Kadburgler, breaking the silence, his smile thin and stiff like usual. He folded his hands neatly in his lap. "I heard your mom went out of town," he began. "Do you need anything while she's gone? Help with dinner, yard work, checking the house at night for disturbances?"

Fraidy hesitated. "How did you... wait, do you know where she went? She went out of town?" His voice cracked, desperation oozing out.

The neighbor's eyes flickered, shoulders tightening. "Oh, word gets around, something about a realtor convention. She seemed pretty excited when I saw her getting into her car this morning. I told her I would make sure you're taken care of while she's gone." An almost mocking smile followed the sentence.

Smarty Pants felt something was off. Why would Mrs. Carver

explain all this to their neighbor but not her own son? He was concerned that Mr. Kadburgler knew more than he was letting on. Wanting to protect his friend, he said, "He's fine. He's staying with me and my parents tonight."

"Ah," Mr. Kadburgler said slowly, his eyes glistening, mustache twitching. "So...the house will be empty?"

Something in his tone made Smarty's stomach churn.

"Actually," he said, "my dad said we could stay here, and he would sleep over too. You know, parental supervision." Smarty Pants chuckled, trying to sound convincing since he wasn't used to lying to adults.

The man's smile twitched under his mustache. "I see." He stood, straightening his neatly pressed shirt. "Well, if you change your mind, I can keep an eye on things. Our windows look right into each other's houses." He peered around, survey-ing the situation. "Just wanting to be neighborly."

"Thanks," Smarty Pants said firmly, trying to claim authority in the conversation.

Mr. Kadburgler nodded once and walked toward the door. The silence that followed was heavy, except for the faint squeak of Mr. Kadburgler's polished shoes. Fraidy was so tense he could hear his heart pounding with anxiety. He couldn't help but feel the need for his mother's warmth now more than ever.

As the neighbor reached for the handle, the house phone rang, loud and sudden.

Unwavering, Mr. Kadburgler turned, his hand still on the doorknob. "You'd better answer that," he said softly.

Then he slipped out, closing the door behind him.

2

The Phone Call

Fraidy Cat was gasping, still recovering from the jump scare of the ringing phone. Smarty Pants, on the other hand, wasn't scared, just frozen, his mind spinning with questions. This day was getting stranger by the second.

The two boys stood motionless until another sharp ring cut through the thick silence.

"I'll get it," Smarty Pants said firmly, trying to calm Fraidy's nerves.

He walked to the long hallway table, crowded with festive decorations. The summer display was a random mix of patriotic colors and a glass bowl of plastic lemons and berries. Next to the decorative bowl sat the house phone. As Smarty Pants reached for it, the phone rang again. Slowly, he grasped the receiver and lifted it to his ear. Fraidy Cat shuffled closer, leaning in to listen, borrowing some of Smarty's courage.

Silence stretched for a moment. Then piercing static emitted through the line. Smarty Pants yanked the phone away, waited, and cautiously returned it to his ringing ear. The static vanished, replaced by a distorted voice.

"Look under the light. Don't trust..."

Then the line went dead.

Smarty Pants' thoughts swirled like a tornado: *Who was that? Why so cryptic? Under what light?* Then, a spark of understanding hit him. *Light... shadows... look beneath the light where shadows play! The note from inside the sandwich!*

While Smarty Pants pieced together the mystery, Fraidy Cat remained paralyzed, haunted by the voice, yet there was something faintly familiar about it.

"Where do shadows play?" Smarty finally asked aloud, grabbing onto the one thought he could hold.

Fraidy Cat didn't respond, his body still stiff like a statue. The only part of him that seemed to be human was his trembling hands, shaking uncontrollably. On a normal day, one sudden noise could scare him, but add the mystery of his mom missing on top of that, and he had become a nervous wreck.

"Fraidy?" Smarty Pants inquired, worried about his friend's mental state. He was hoping that reminding him of the note would give him something else to focus on. "Do you know where shadows play?"

Smarty placed a comforting hand on Fraidy's shoulder, feeling the tension leaving his body under the weight of his warm hand. Returning his attention back to the present, Fraidy slowly inhaled and exhaled, trying to steady his hands.

"I didn't know shadows could play," Fraidy said, while clasping his hands, forcing them to remain still. "Aren't they stuck to us? They can't just wander off and play by themselves." His voice trembled, a shiver washing over his body. Ever since finding the first note from his mom, he'd felt like someone, or something, was watching him. In this particular moment, he felt as though he were under a microscope, the invisible watcher's eyes so intense.

"You're right," Smarty Pants said, mystified. "Maybe it's not the shadows. Maybe they just mark the time of day. So it must mean when it's dark out, or the sun is gone. And it's near a light..."

Voice trailing off, Smarty Pants was trying really hard to do his best thinking under the stress of the situation.

"The only shadows I remember are ours, running and playing soccer in the backyard when it gets dark," Fraidy said, smiling at the memory of safer times. Times of his mom watching over him, rather than the unknown stranger he felt watching him now.

"The backyard! The light in the backyard! Let's go!" Smarty Pants grabbed Fraidy's arm and pulled him toward the kitchen. Knowing it was useless to resist, Fraidy followed behind, thankful for this distraction. Quickly, they sped through the kitchen, passing the scent of the stale sandwich that still sat on the table. The familiar screech of the sliding glass door welcomed them into the cool night air.

At the end of the backyard, a tall lamp post stood guard. After the many nose bleeds and shin scrapes from the boys bumping and tripping while playing soccer in the dark, Fraidy's mom had installed the light. She would sit on the patio, watching the boys chase the ball, their shadows whirling alongside them.

The boys rushed to the lamp, the bright beam revealing a disturbed patch of dirt at the base that they might have otherwise missed. They clawed at the earth, too impatient to find shovels, the scent of fresh soil infiltrated their noses.

Clink!

A sharp noise echoed as fingernails hit metal. They froze, eyes meeting in silent celebration. Smarty Pants scraped again, and there it was, the corner of a small metal box glinting in the lamplight. Like archaeologists, they extracted their treasure from the earth.

Smarty Pants picked up the cold metal box, relief replacing the ache in his hands. He remained stunned in disbelief, staring at his prize resting in his hands. He was excited to follow the clues and solve the riddle, but he didn't think it would actually end with him holding buried treasure. Just as he moved to open it, Fraidy's hands pressed down on his, stopping him. He couldn't see anyone watching them, but he could feel it, and he wanted to protect their loot from the watcher's invisible gaze.

"Let's open it inside," Fraidy said cautiously, still uneasy. Smarty Pants nodded, and they headed back toward the sliding door. As Fraidy turned to close the sliding glass door after entering the safety of his kitchen, a small rustle came from the branches beyond the shared fence of Fraidy Cat and Mr. Kadburgler though the air was still.

Fraidy glanced closer, trying to see who was out there with them, but Smarty Pants exhale of excitement drew him back. Making the quick decision of investigating with Smarty rather than exploring the dark outdoors alone, Fraidy remained inside, sliding the glass door closed and latching the lock. With the door shut, the boys set the treasure on the kitchen countertop, staring in awe, their discovery safe from prying eyes.

Before them was a small metal box. There was nothing special about it. It was simple in design, just a metal square container with a matching metal lid. However, this was the same box that Fraidy Cat would see every morning. This box typically housed Q-tips in the bathroom, but now it was covered with dirt, holding unknown secrets. Seeing this familiar box led Fraidy Cat to believe that his mom really did bury it, but why?

As they opened the small box, tiny flecks of dirt rained down on the once clean hardwood floors. Inside was a little key, bronzed with age, dangling from a long matching chain. Fraidy turned it over in his fingers, studying every angle, wondering what secrets this key unlocked, knowing he had seen the key somewhere before. Smarty Pants grasped the other item in the box, a clean folded sheet of paper. He unfolded the paper, the smooth edges gliding over his dirty hands. A smaller, aged fragment of paper was embedded in the folds. When it was released from its hiding place, it fell to the floor, drifting softly. Fraidy picked it up, while Smarty Pants began to read the folded paper aloud:

"If you found this, the danger was closer than I thought. Keep the key safe. Trust only James."

Standing up with the fragment in his hands, Fraidy Cat peered over at the note Smarty Pants was holding. Fraidy's eyes widened as he recognized his mom's handwriting, the same handwriting from the riddle in the sandwich. This note confirmed his worst fear: he was all alone and his mom was in trouble.

Seeing Fraidy's worry, Smarty Pants placed a reassuring hand on his friend's shoulder. With all the confidence he could muster, he said, "We're going to find her. I promise."

3

The Scrap of Truth

Exhausted from the mysterious day, Smarty Pants rested on the floor in his usual spot on top of a foam pad and a few blankets, right on the side of Fraidy Cat's bed. As he laid there, he looked up at the ceiling, seeing all the animals he had deciphered in the textured ceiling many nights before, the lion being his favorite. However, those nights were not plagued with the worries that filled the air in Fraidy Cat's bedroom tonight.

Fraidy Cat sat upright in his bed, twirling the scrap of paper that had fallen out of the metal box, still trying to figure out what it could mean. It appeared to be a news article that was written many years ago. The color of the page had faded from a once bright white to a pale yellow; the paper now soft with age, creases abundant on its once smooth surface. After a few more twirls, Fraidy read the fragment again, hoping some new information would be revealed.

E FORTUNE IN ABANDONED MINE
hers Elias and Edwin Carver, both
long-closed Maple Hollow Mine,
e calling the largest diamond

No matter how many times he read this small fragment, he was still lost in confusion and desperate for his mom to walk through his bedroom door. The only thing he knew for certain was that this wasn't a random piece of paper, there was meaning behind this discovery. Edwin Carver was Fraidy's great-great-grandfather.

"I think we should go to the library tomorrow. Look into Maple Hollow Mine," Smarty Pants blurted aloud, making a mental checklist. "They have this really cool book there that goes into detail about the town's and mine's history."

"The library, I'm fine with that, just as long as we stay far away from that haunted mine," Fraidy said with a visible shiver from mentioning the mine, recalling the last time he had been there. They were younger, and being scared of everything, Smarty Pants thought it would be funny to dare him to touch the wood planks covering the mine opening. Fraidy didn't even get within arm's reach before he ran away, swearing he saw something move inside.

"It's all just a ghost story", Smarty Pants chuckled. "It's not really haunted. There is nothing living in the mine but bugs and maybe a few bats."

"Ghosts, bats, bugs, I'm good never meeting anything that calls that mine home," Fraidy Cat declared. "I am ok with going to the library, but going to that mine is off the table."

Smarty Pants laughed at Fraidy Cat being so dramatic. "Why? It's your great-great-grandpa involved in this news article. He has something to do with the mine and your mom is leading us to him. Don't you want to find out what she is leading us to? See how Edwin fits in with her disappearance? You could walk his footsteps and we could solve this mystery and find your mom!"

A thick pause filled the air. Fraidy Cat knew that there were real stakes involved in this mystery. However, he got carried away with his fears of the mine and the creatures that called it home.

"You don't think she is in the mine, do you?" Fraidy leaned over the edge of the bed to look Smarty Pants in the eyes. Worry was written all over his face.

"No. Your mom is safe. Maybe she is just hiding. Don't worry. I promised we will find her."

With that promise, Fraidy returned his head to his pillow, pulled the covers up to his face, and closed his eyes, thinking of yesterday when his mom came in to tell him goodnight. Smarty Pants, on the other hand, laid with his eyes wide open, his mind trying to solve the case so he could keep his promise.

The sunlight trickled in through the curtains and landed on Fraidy's forehead, waking him gently from his sleep. He quickly sat up, hoping yesterday was just a nightmare, but he felt the cold chain and key pressing against his chest. He looked over and on his bedside table laid the small fragment of an old newspaper, and Fraidy Cat knew that this wasn't a nightmare, it was his reality.

He climbed over the bottom of his bed, knowing what floorboards to avoid because their creaks would disturb the silence in his room. As he made his way out of his bedroom door, he found himself wandering down the hallway. His mom's bedroom door was open. The pain of seeing her empty bed caused him to feel an emotion he didn't know he felt: anger. He was angry that he was alone. Angry that she left him. Then guilt rushed through his body. He shouldn't be angry at his mom. He didn't want to be angry. He quickly grabbed her door handle and shut it tight, hoping to also shut out his anger.

As he turned his back on the shut door, he found himself looking at another open door, this time it was to his mom's office. As he sighed looking inside, debating whether entering was a good idea, he finally placed a foot into the room. As he tread past open house signs and bookcases filled with his mom's favorite stories and realtor awards, he realized he had never been in this room without her before. He missed her. As he rounded her large wooden desk, he climbed up into her dark leather computer chair, pretending it was a hug that he was so desperately craving.

As the chair slowly spun, he saw a picture on the wall of two men wearing overalls and headlamps. He remembered sitting with his dad on the office floor, playing army men while his mom worked at the desk. He remembered his dad noticed he was staring at the photo.

That's my great-grandpa Edwin and his brother Elias. They used to be miners here in Pine City, his dad explained to him.

His dad was excited to share this bit of family history, however, young Fraidy Cat only wanted to play with his dad and didn't want the history lesson. Six years later, he now regretted this choice. He wished his dad could be here to help him find his mom; to tell him about his family history.

All he knew was that this picture used to represent bravery and adventure; now, when he caught the glimpse of it, mystery, intrigue, and a bit of anger washed over him. Anger again, he wished he could get rid of it.

He slid off of his mother's office chair, the back of his thighs slightly sticking to the leather in his pajama shorts. As he made his way over to the picture, his heart was thudding hard in his chest, praying that this would hold the answers. But when he got there, it was just a picture. There was no note written on it; no new clue to follow.

"Find anything?"

Fraidy Cat lived up to his name. He jumped so high off the ground, he looked like a cartoon character that had jumped out of his skin.

"Sorry," Smarty Pants said with a small laugh. "I didn't mean to scare you." He never meant to startle Fraidy Cat, but it was a funny coincidence when it happened, which was often.

Trying to catch his breath, Fraidy Cat responded through his panting, "No... I just... saw this picture... it's my... it's my... Great-great-grandpa, Edwin and his brother."

Smarty Pants approached the picture frame. They were both staring at the picture intently, hoping Elias or Edwin would start talking and tell them what was going on, but they never did. Then, Smarty Pants' eyes caught hold of the antique frame that was housing the picture and it was covered in dust, except in one corner of the frame.

Smarty Pants reached out and snatched the frame off the wall. Fraidy Cat stood there, frozen, confused by what was happening but knew not to interfere when Smarty Pants had an idea.

Smarty Pants made his way over to the office desk, flipped the picture over and looked at its back. He could see the recent pry marks at the backing with a paper hanging out. This paper was a pale yellow color which increased his urgency. Picking up the letter opener that was lying on the desk, Smarty Pants gently lifted each metal tab that was holding the backing in place. After completely removing the back, which seemed to have taken hours, the boys were stunned. They were left staring at what should have been the back of the photo of Elias and Edwin Carver, but instead was the remaining news article that was a perfect puzzle piece to the scrap that they had found in the metal box last night.

Fraidy Cat slowly and timidly reached for the larger piece of the news article, careful not to rip it in its fragile state, and laid it out on the desk. By the time he had placed it down, Smarty Pants had returned from the bedroom with the smaller fragment.

Smarty Pants placed the smaller fragment next to the larger paper, and it was a perfect fit. With a small amount of tape from a dispenser next to a framed picture of Fraidy and his mom at the zoo, the news article was complete. Smarty Pants held it up and they both pressed their heads near each other to read the mystery that they both dreamt about last night.

4

The Legend Unearthed

LOCAL TWINS STRIKE FORTUNE IN ABANDONED MINE

In a twist of fate, twin brothers Elias and Edwin Carver, both former miners of the recently closed Maple Hollow Mine, stumbled upon what experts are calling the largest diamond ever found on American soil.

The discovery came during a return visit to the site, where the brothers sought to recover tools left behind after the sudden mine's closure last winter. Amidst deserted beams and rubble, Elias reportedly noticed a faint shimmer beneath the dust, a gem so large and pure that one witness described it as *"a piece of the sun trapped in stone."*

The remarkable jewel, quickly dubbed The Mother Diamond, is said to bring luck to any who glimpse its glow in sunlight. The brothers have sworn to keep the diamond within the Carver family until it can be properly secured and displayed for all to see. "It's a gift," said Edwin Carver, "and gifts like this must be shared, not sold."

The brothers declined to disclose the exact location of the find, citing safety concerns at the abandoned site.

As soon as Smarty Pants finished reading the news article aloud, he suddenly bolted for the door, leaving Fraidy Cat sitting in stunned silence.

"Where are you going?" Fraidy Cat called after him, confusion lacing his voice. He could hear Smarty Pants calling from the bathroom with his reply.

"To... (*spit*)... get to the... (*spit*)... library!" Smarty Pants said through a toothbrush scraping his teeth. After he had properly rinsed his mouth, he called back, "I've got so many questions, and there's no time to waste!"

Within minutes, both boys had changed their clothes, combed their hair, and pulled on their shoes. Smarty Pants brought his backpack too, just in case they found an interesting book. They got ready faster than if they were late to school; Smarty Pants was excited about this study session and Fraidy Cat was eager to get closer to finding his mom.

As they stepped outside, Fraidy Cat paused, the uneasy feeling of being watched creeping over him again. He hadn't had this feeling all morning and was hoping it had vanished with the night. Realizing this sensation was sticking around, he quickly locked the door, hoping the click of the latch would calm the flutter in his chest. However, it didn't leave. He felt more exposed away from his house. He wanted nothing more than to climb into his bed and hide under the covers, but he knew he had to be brave. Or at least pretend to be.

Hurrying down Fraidy Cat's front porch steps, the boys quickly made their way to the side of the house, next to the garage. Standing on their kickstands with their helmets hanging off the handlebars, the boys' most prize possessions were waiting for them: their bikes. After the click of their helmets from under their chins, they each swung a leg around the frame of their bike, quickly pressing on a pedal. As they took off from the driveway, they passed rows of houses that all looked the same. However, each house had a slightly different variation; one with a red door, some with a second garage, and others with an attic big enough to be a third floor.

The breeze from their bike ride to the library was refreshing. For a few fleeting moments, Fraidy Cat felt like a regular kid again, one whose world wasn't falling apart, whose mom would be home waiting with a warm hug. Fraidy Cat clung to this momentary feeling, hoping that it would soon return for good. For Smarty Pants, the wind felt like pure adventure. He could practically taste discovery on the air. He didn't like the cause of this mystery, but he was enjoying the journey.

When they skidded to a stop and parked their bikes, Smarty Pants was already fumbling for his library card. This was one of his most prized possessions, right up there with his bike. Smarty never went anywhere without his library card and it showed. The barcode almost rubbed from over use. The library was his favorite place. It was quiet, predictable, and filled with answers to his questions.

Fraidy Cat still felt vulnerable outside, but he was trying not to let it show. But no matter how much he tried to push his worries down, he kept wishing he could be back at home, especially if his mom came home while he was gone.

Smarty Pants led the way straight to the local history section, weaving through the aisles like he'd been born there. Fraidy Cat trailed behind, glancing through the narrow gaps between bookshelves. The books on the shelves slowly started to blur, his mom consuming his thoughts.

Movement behind a stack of books caught Fraidy Cat's eye. Was it the watcher again? He couldn't shake the feeling that someone, or something, was still watching him. However, when he peered closer, looking over a thick book, no one was there. The absence of the watcher was an even more terrifying thought than discovering their identity.

Streaming his finger along the spines of the books, Smarty Pants felt like a pirate searching for his gold. "Here it is!" he shouted, earning a chorus of *shhh*s from the surrounding readers. He lowered his voice. "A book about the mining boom days of Pine City. Too bad this couldn't have happened next year. The city is supposed to have all these books online within the year."

Fraidy Cat smiled in amazement at his friend. He should have known that Smarty Pants would be up to date on the current events of the library. Also, Smarty Pants didn't look too sad about the book not being online yet. He would use any excuse to take a trip to the library.

Smarty Pants carried the heavy volume to a dusty reading nook with a beanbag chair that smelled faintly of age and mystery. As they both settled in, the air released a puff of dust and the faint tang of moldy paper floated into the air.

The boys read eagerly about Maple Hollow Mine, once the pride of Pine City employing most of its townsfolk. It had been owned by one of the wealthiest families in town, but misfortune struck when the family's patriarch gambled away their wealth. The mine was shut down shortly after.

Elias and Edwin Carver had been miners there. When the mine closed suddenly, they'd left their tools behind. Weeks later, they returned to retrieve them. That's when the ground began to shake. The brothers feared a cave-in, but as the earth settled and dust filled the air, the flicker of Elias's headlamp caught a blinding glimmer deep in the rock.

When the rumbling stopped, Elias brushed away the dirt and saw it: the biggest diamond he had ever imagined.

At the mention of the diamond, Smarty Pants and Fraidy Cat exchanged a wide-eyed look. Could this be the reason for his mother's disappearance? Did someone think she was in possession of the diamond now?

Fraidy Cat's worries were beginning to boil over. He came to the library for answers, not more questions. He couldn't believe he left the safety of his home for this. He just wanted to be back home again.

"I wonder if Mom has more information on Elias and Edwin in her office," Fraidy Cat whispered, hoping to steer Smarty Pants back toward home, the one place he still felt safe.

Smarty Pants took the hint and closed the book, he was feeling a bit hungry and didn't need much persuasion. As they headed for the checkout desk, Fraidy Cat felt a tap on his shoulder. He turned, heart hammering.

It was Mr. Kadburgler. His familiar mustache bounced as he smiled at them.

"So, how was your night? No parental supervision, I see," he said, his tone light but his gaze sharp.

"My dad ended up sleeping over with us but he left early this morning. He got called into work," Smarty Pants replied quickly. "But he was with us all night." He held his shoulders proudly, rather than considering this lying he thought of it more as being undercover.

"That's good," Mr. Kadburgler said, straightening out his collar. "Always nice to have someone keeping an eye on you. Interested in our town's history, are you?" He nodded toward the book clutched tightly in Smarty Pants' hands.

"School project," Fraidy Cat blurted, proud of his quick thinking.

"Isn't it summer?" Mr. Kadburgler asked, raising an eyebrow.

Fraidy Cat's shoulders sank, realizing his mistake. He felt defeated. If he couldn't even get this right, how was he going to save his mom? He wished he was more like Smarty Pants.

"Extra credit," Smarty Pants jumped in smoothly. "The teacher said it'll give us a head start for next year." Both boys smiled at this excuse. Smarty Pants smiled because he was proud of his quick response, Fraidy Cat because he was so thankful that Smarty Pants was his friend.

Mr. Kadburgler chuckled softly. "Aren't you two good little students?" At this, he patted Fraidy on the head like a dog, sending a disgusted wave through his body. "Well, Freddy, if you need anything while your mom's away, my offer still stands. I can keep an eye on the house."

Before either of the boys could respond, he turned and left the library empty-handed, leaving behind the faint smell of his heavily applied cologne.

5

The Chest of Secrets

As the boys rounded the corner into Fraidy Cat's neighborhood, they sped up; Smarty Pants' backpack was bouncing against his back, heavy with the library book. The boys were eager to keep reading about the diamond and its connection to the Carver family, wondering if this was the reason Fraidy Cat's mom was missing. Smarty Pants enjoyed the myth and mystery, but Fraidy Cat was hoping it would lead to his mom. When they finally arrived at Fraidy Cat's house and up the driveway, they jumped off their bikes, the metal frames clattering against the ground.

Smarty Pants ran for the door, taking giant strides. However, Fraidy glanced back to make sure his bike was still in one piece then froze, petrified.

Next door, Mr. Kadburgler stood on his porch, peering over at Fraidy Cat's house, mug in hand. He gave a slow, deliberate wave that sent a chill down Fraidy's spine.

Fraidy gave a quick, polite wave back, then hurried to meet Smarty Pants at the front door.

"He's really starting to creep me out," Fraidy muttered as he fumbled with the house key.

"Yeah. He's talked to us more in the last two days than in the whole time you've lived here," Smarty Pants said, glancing over his shoulder. "Why does he keep *watching* you like that?"

"I don't know, but he usually keeps to himself ever since he moved in a couple years ago. Only comes over if he accidentally gets our mail or needs to borrow something."

They both turned for one last look. Mr. Kadburgler was still staring, investigating their every move. Quickly, the boys slipped inside and locked the door tight behind them, sliding the deadbolt just to be sure.

As they peered out the curtained windows, making sure that Mr. Kadburgler wasn't going to follow them over, a loud grumble filled the quiet lonely house. With a small chuckle from Smarty Pants, Fraidy Cat quickly grabbed his stomach out of embarrassment. Recognizing their need for food, they both headed into the kitchen.

They quickly went to work piling up their snacks, potato chips, pastries, soda pop. Surveying their loot, Fraidy Cat felt a little guilty and grabbed a banana too, knowing it would make his mom happy.

Arms full of snacks, they settled in the living room, determined to finish reading about the Mother Diamond and the Carver family. Smarty Pants opened the dusty book from the library and continued reading aloud.

After the Mother Diamond's discovery, Elias and Edwin Carver debated what to do with it. Legally, the diamond belonged to them because the mine had closed already, and no one else could claim it. But morally, the brothers felt it was too great a treasure to keep. They wanted to share its beauty with the town.

Eventually the brothers had the stone cut and polished, the product of it being larger than a softball.

After keeping the precious stone safe themselves for years, Edwin became curator of the local museum and secured a safe place for the diamond to be displayed for the whole town to appreciate it.

Word of the Mother Diamond being on display spread and people came from all over to see her. Some said sunlight through the diamond brought them luck. Others swore it healed their ailments. Thus the legend of the Mother Diamond grew.

One morning, after a year of the diamond being on display, a note was found pinned to the museum doors.

"The true owner will return for what is rightfully theirs."

The Carver brothers were shaken, but they refused to remove the diamond from display. Edwin Carver was repeatedly insisting that the diamond was meant to be shared and that the security measures that were in place would ensure the safety of the Mother Diamond.

However, within a week, it was gone. All that remained was a scrap of paper lying in the empty case.

"The Mother has come home."
The whole town was devastated, but none more than the Carver brothers who refused to comment after the theft.

"It's gone…" Fraidy Cat whispered, feeling this small strand of hope to find his mom shatter into tiny bits.

"Not gone," Smarty Pants interjected, though his voice wavered. "Just in a new place. We'll find it. We just need more clues." He paused. "Where does your mom keep the old photo albums and family stuff?"

"She keeps them upstairs in her office. There's a whole chest full of stuff she inherited from the Carver side when my dad passed away."

Closing the heavy book, they cleaned up their snack mess, a banana peel resting on top of the pile. Not usually good at keeping things tidy, Fraidy Cat wanted to make sure the house was clean if—no, when his mom came home.

After cleaning up as best they could, they crept up the creaky stairs, each step groaning beneath their weight. They passed a closet door, Fraidy's bedroom door, then the bathroom door, but when they reached the closed door near the end of the hall, Fraidy Cat stopped and stared at it intently, his fingers going numb with pain.

Fraidy's mom's bedroom door was still closed. Fraidy longed for his mom to walk out that door right now and tell him that everything was okay, but she couldn't; she was still missing. A comforting hand rested on Fraidy's shoulder. This one gesture was enough to reinforce the promise that Smarty Pants had made to find his mom.

With a small amount of guiding, they turned to face the opposite side of the hall where the office was. The smell of old leather and plastic 'for sale' signs filled the room. A large wooden chest waited near the window, heavy with dust and secrets.

They stood on either side of the chest, clutching the antique handles, and lifted the lid. A soft puff of dust rose, dancing in the sunlight. Coughing, they wafted the air, clearing the particles that invaded their airways.

Peering inside, they saw stacks of old photographs filled with various vacations, wedding days, and some first days of school. The photos began to fade from bright color to black and white, bringing the feeling of older times. Shuffling through the third stack of photos, at last, they found a picture of two men who shared the same face. Twins.

Hope rising in them, they continued digging deeper, praying that another artifact from the twins would surface, one that hinted toward a secret discovery. At the bottom of the chest lay a brown journal with worn corners that had once gleamed gold.

As Fraidy reached for the journal, the edges of the chest dug into his skin. Reaching further, the key around his neck pressed into his chest. Memories of the night before flooded his mind, all returning to the question of what this key unlocked? Why was it so important? Why did it look so familiar, like a distant memory? Then came the ache of missing his mom but he forced himself to push it down and lifted the journal out.

Placing the journal on the carpeted rug, Fraidy stood back, fearful of the path it could lead them on, hoping it wouldn't lead them farther away from his mom. Smarty Pants, eager to continue the mystery, gently opened it. On the inside cover, in faded blue ink, was written: *Edwin Carver.*

They looked at each other and smiled, feeling as though they had just unearthed the Mother Diamond itself. Carefully flipping through the fragile pages, Smarty Pants found an entry about the diamond's discovery, then read about displaying it at the museum.

"It says Elias was furious that Edwin put the diamond on display," Smarty read. "He thought something bad would happen."

"I guess he was right," Fraidy said softly. "If they hadn't brought it there, it wouldn't have been stolen."

"Elias and Edwin never spoke again once the Mother Diamond was stolen," Smarty continued, saddened at the thought of never talking to a family member again. "Not until Elias was on his deathbed."

"I hope they made up," Fraidy murmured. "I can't imagine being that mad at someone, especially your own brother."

"You're the closest thing I've got to a brother," Smarty Pants said, trying to sound casual, but his voice cracked. "I couldn't go a day without talking to you."

"Same! We *are* brothers," Fraidy said firmly. "Who else would help me through all this?"

They shared a grin before Smarty turned the page again. Both boys were stunned.

Their eyes darted up to meet each other, the words on the page astounding them.

"Elias knew who took the diamond," Fraidy whispered in confusion.

"And he told Edwin," Smarty said, finishing their shared thought.

6

The Last Page

With the journal spread between them, Smarty Pants and Fraidy Cat read page after page, growing more confused with each sentence. At the beginning of the journal, Edwin's handwriting had been neat, proper, and easy to follow. But toward the end of it, the words became frantic scribbles, sentences half-formed, lines twisting in circles, punctuation disappearing entirely.

Randomly placed within the chaotic penmanship was a hand-drawn image of a key on a long chain, the same one that was now resting around Fraidy Cat's neck. The room fell silent, not even their breathing could be heard. Then Fraidy Cat quickly pulled his hand to his chest, feeling the key and chain beneath it and remembering; he had seen this key and chain before.

He scrambled to his feet, falling toward his mom's office desk. As he caught hold of the edge of the desk, he reached his other arm across it and grabbed a picture frame. Five-year-old Fraidy Cat was smiling back up at Fraidy now. The younger version of him was sitting in his mother's lap with his father standing behind them. As he looked closer, he could see the aged chain peeking out of his father's shirt and wrapping around his neck.

"It was his…" Fraidy Cat stammered.

"What was his?" Smarty Pants questioned, seeing the photo Fraidy was holding and knowing that his dad was a sensitive subject.

"This key around my neck," Fraidy Cat pulled at the chain, digging it into his hand, "it was my dad's. Why would my mom bury it? What does all of this have to do with the Carvers?"

Smarty Pants sighed and paused to think. "I don't know the answers to those questions, but I do know this: we are on the right track. If your mom wanted you to find that key, if your dad wore it around his neck, then it must be important. And now that key is in this journal; we are getting closer. I just know this is going to lead us to your mom."

Fraidy Cat brought the picture up to his sight line again, staring at the happy family. Looking at his dad, it hurt. He missed him every day. But looking at his mom, that was a different pain; it was unresolved. He had to get back on the case and focus for her. He had to find her.

He set the frame back on the desk, but this time, he left the photo facing them; hoping his dad was watching over them.

Fraidy Cat walked over to their center of operations and found his spot on the ground again. He gave Smarty Pants a nervous, but confident smile and signaled to him that they could continue reading the journal.

The remaining pages were filled with warnings: whispers from the stone, eyes that followed him, and Edwin blaming both himself and Elias. Through all the confusion and questions, Fraidy Cat and Smarty Pants knew one thing for certain; these were the etchings of a madman.

When they finally reached the last page, they froze. The handwriting returned to neat script, but the words were cryptic:

"When the light glows blue, choose one or two. If you choose right, it will be your last night. When you approach the gate, give it the answer to learn your fate."

Below this message was a scrawled line that twisted and turned with no apparent rhyme or reason. The clean and clear riddle seemed out of place among the scribbles that occupied the remaining space, leaving nothing else on the page legible.

"Well, that settles it," Smarty Pants said, his voice full of determination.

"Settles what? That my great-great-grandfather was obsessed with the Mother Diamond and lost his mind?" Fraidy Cat joked nervously, trying to ease his anxiety.

"No. I mean yes, but no. We need to go to the mine! We have to see if the riddle fits."

"No! You promised we would never go back there after you double-dog dared me in third grade."

"I know, but this is for your mom. All our clues are leading us there."

Fraidy Cat felt a small amount of betrayal from his best friend. If he hadn't forced him to go there when he was younger, then he wouldn't be scared now. It was his fault he was terrified of the mine and the bats that chased him away. But, Smarty Pants was right. He had to be brave for his mom, or at least pretend to be brave.

"Fine... but I'm staying outside," he relented. "I'll be on lookout duty."

With that, the plan was set in motion. They packed their backpacks: flashlights, head lamps, notebooks, rope, jackets, and the necessary bag of potato chips. Smarty Pants hesitantly called his parents, thinking it was best to ask their permission. When neither answered, he left a vague voicemail on their house phone, letting them know they went to ride their bikes on the mountain. Leaving the safety of the house and returning to the fresh air, the boys mounted their bikes, grateful for their form of transportation and the freedom it brought them. A bike ride to the mine rather than walking would save them hours.

As they pedaled, the familiar rows of houses faded behind them, replaced by dense trees. The sounds of cars were gone, in their place were chirping birds and leaves rustling in the wind. Each hill they climbed up brought them closer to the mine, and the boys' anticipation grew. Sweat was beading off the boys' faces, but Fraidy's was more so out of fear. Fear was making his body ache, but he pushed through it with each pedal, repeating *anything for mom* in his head.

The entrance to the mine was barricaded with rotting wood. Etched on their surface were faded warnings: *Danger! Keep Out!* The decay had left a large enough opening for the boys to squeeze through, but only one had the courage to enter.

"You can wait here. I'll be back soon," Smarty Pants told Fraidy Cat, hoping he would reconsider, but he was not going to push the matter knowing how fearful he was about the mine.

"I'll be right here," Fraidy Cat replied, pretending to be confident.

Fraidy Cat watched as Smarty Pants squeezed through the small opening in the mine. Smarty Pants looked back at Fraidy, desperate for him to join him, but putting on a brave face. He gave his friend a weak smile, then disappeared into the darkness of the mine.

Alone.

Fraidy Cat stood there, facing the mine entrance, completely alone. He studied his surroundings. The wood surrounding the mine was rotting with age, some planks missing chunks of wood. The rock mountainside was adorned with wildflowers, giving a softness to the jagged edges of the boulders. The trees were a nice blend of aspens and pine trees.

Crunch!

Fraidy Cat quickly turned around, but saw nothing in the direction the noise came from. The feeling of being watched gnawed at him once again. He was hoping that by getting away from town, the eyes that followed him would too be left behind. However, they seemed to peer into his soul now, away from civilization. Then he remembered Smarty Pants was in the cave and he was alone. Alone with his watcher.

He felt every muscle in his body tense, his jaw clenched with his lip stuck between his teeth. Before he realized what he was doing, he found himself squeezing through the gap in the planks, entering the mine.

It didn't take long to catch up to Smarty Pants, their beams of flashlights meeting up with each other.

"I thought you were keeping watch," Smarty Pants said, startled but grateful for the company.

"I realized you might need backup... and I didn't want to be alone," Fraidy Cat admitted.

"Honestly, I'm glad you came. I didn't want to be alone either."

The boys moved deeper into the tunnel, their flashlights slicing through the darkness. The air smelled of damp earth and stone. Small rocks trickled down the walls, echoing through the empty tunnels.

"This is hopeless," Fraidy Cat whispered, uneasy about the thought of a cave-in.

"Wait, what's over there?" Smarty Pants asked, moving closer to a glowing section of the rock wall.

Specks of blue shimmered across the tunnel, and then the entire passage seemed to glow blue. Ahead, the tunnel forked into two paths. *Choose one or two* echoed in Smarty Pants' mind.

He stepped forward, but Fraidy Cat grabbed his arm, stopping him before he made a choice.

"What if we choose the wrong way and get lost forever?" Fraidy Cat whispered, panic rising.

"Well, what do you think we should do?" Smarty Pants asked, unsure of the correct answer, trying to remain calm.

Fraidy's breathing began to shorten. He felt like he couldn't take a breath as his heart pounded in his chest. "I... I can't choose! I want to get out of here!" Fraidy Cat shouted in a panic, forgetting to whisper. The earth trembled slightly, just enough to terrify the boys.

Panic fueling him, Fraidy Cat led the way back through the tunnel, trying to make the least amount of noise possible with each step, praying that a cave-in wouldn't make this their grave. Smarty Pants followed behind, again, grateful for the company.

When they emerged into the fresh air, the sun was dipping

toward the horizon. They started for their bikes, ready to ride home.

The bikes were gone. If they hadn't been panicking before, they definitely were now. They felt deserted.

Alone.

Except those invisible watching eyes.

Fraidy Cat scanned the trees nervously, sensing them. Wanting to find them, but wishing they would leave.

Smarty Pants inspected the ground and saw bike tire tracks that led away, then abruptly stopped. The bikes had vanished as if they had disappeared into the sky.

"I guess we better start walking," Smarty Pants said, glancing at the setting sun and running out of options.

Smarty Pants began their long journey, Fraidy Cat closing the distance between them. Together, they headed down the hill, hoping the remaining daylight would guide their path, but knowing soon, they would be alone in the dark, with the watcher's eyes following their every move.

For somewhere deeper in the woods, a shadow moved silently. It paused, studying the boys from just beyond the edge of sight, before disappearing into the trees.

Neither Smarty Pants nor Fraidy Cat noticed it.

Not yet.

7

The Watcher in the Dark

The sunlight was fading faster than the boys could move their tired feet down the rocky mountain trail. What felt like miles stretched on endlessly, though they hadn't even made it halfway home. With each step came the crunch of leaves and shuffle of dirt beneath their sneakers, but sometimes Fraidy Cat thought he could hear those same sounds coming from behind them. Following them.

"So, Mr. Detective," Fraidy Cat stammered, trying not to sound as alarmed as he felt, obsessively cracking his knuckles to relieve some anxiety. "Who do you think took our bikes? And more importantly, why would someone take them?"

Smarty Pants stayed quiet, eyes fixed ahead, thinking through every possibility.

"Maybe someone's watching us," he finally said. "Maybe they think we're getting too close to finding the Mother Diamond or even your mom. Maybe they want us to stop looking and they'll do anything to make sure that happens." Mind racing, he was exciting himself with these possible solutions and the mystery at hand.

Fraidy Cat gulped, loudly, startling resting birds in a nearby tree. Smarty Pants eyed his friend, seeing fear rushing through him.

"Or," he added quickly, "maybe it's just some kids playing a prank."

But even as he said it, Smarty Pants knew his voice didn't sound very convincing. Why would someone be up here at this time of day? Why would they take their bikes? It had to be something more malicious, he just didn't want to fully admit it.

They trudged on silently, fearful of where that last conversation got them. The sun melted into the horizon, leaving only a blanket of darkness. Every so often, Fraidy Cat heard a branch snap or leaves rustle behind him, but every time he quickly turned his head to scan the tree line, nothing was there.

Until there was.

A shadowy figure stood among the bushes not far behind them. Fraidy Cat froze, fear rooting him to the spot. Smarty Pants continued walking along the path toward home before he realized that Fraidy Cat was no longer next to him. Peering behind himself to find his friend, he saw that Fraidy Cat was motionless, staring intensely into the trees just beyond them. Following Fraidy Cat's gaze, Smarty Pants locked eyes with the same dark silhouette.

Contrary to Fraidy Cat's response, he didn't freeze; instead, he sprung to life. He charged at the figure that had plagued their every movement.

Smarty Pants took giant strides toward the silhouette. As he gained on the watcher, his foot slid off a rock that was on the dirt path. His ankle buckled under his weight, taking Smarty Pants down to the ground. Knowing he did not have time to evaluate his injury, he jumped back up, trying his best to run toward the direction of where the watcher had been, but his jog looked more like a hobble. When Smarty Pants finally reached the spot the watcher had been, the figure had already vanished into the darkness that swallowed the mountainside.

When Fraidy Cat saw his friend stumble, it pulled him out of his paralysis. He quickly moved to where Smarty Pants was on the ground. Before he could reach him though, Smarty Pants was already rushing toward the watcher again. Fraidy Cat lightly jogged behind Smarty Pants, concerned for his friend, but also not wanting to be alone.

The boys were left standing in the heavy silence, the only sounds were of them panting. Fraidy Cat frantically fidgeted with his flashlight, hoping to shine a light in the trees to catch the watcher. Smarty Pants scanned around them, but when he saw nothing, bent down to tend to his ankle. It was red and swollen, heat emitting from it. As he sat on the floor, relieving the pressure he was putting on his injury, he saw something imprinted in the dirt next to him.

"Shine your light over here Fraidy!" Smarty Pants called out to his friend.

When the light landed on the spot Smarty Pants instructed, there were no disturbed branches, no torn clothing. Just two shoe prints pressed into the dirt. Within those shoe prints, a single word written in each: *Bawden.*

To Fraidy Cat, it might as well have been a foreign language; the word *Bawden* had no important significance to him. But to Smarty Pants, it was something more. This meant they finally had a clue to who was behind their bikes going missing, and maybe even Fraidy Cat's mom disappearing. This meant the watcher could be traced, his identity revealed.

Before they could say anything, two headlights glared through the darkness. A loud, familiar engine rumbled toward them.

"Dad!" Smarty Pants sighed in relief, unaware of how fearful of the watcher he really had been.

Andrew rolled down the window, his voice booming. "I've been looking everywhere for you two! Get in!"

Sensing the worry in his voice, the boys didn't hesitate. They dove into the back seat, grateful for the warmth and the safety of the car.

"Where are your bikes?" Andrew Shelley asked the boys in the back seat.

"I think they were stolen. We just left them alone for a little bit, but when we came back, they were gone." Smarty Pants sighed at the thought. He was genuinely sad that they were gone.

"What were you two doing up here anyways?" Andrew asked as he turned the car around.

"We were…" he started, but the pain in his ankle caught up to him, and his words trailed off.

"Exploring!" Fraidy Cat blurted, his voice high and nervous. Smarty Pants blinked but decided to roll with it.

"Exploring?" Andrew repeated, clearly confused.

Smarty Pants jumped in. "We found some books about the history of Pine City and wanted to see some of the places in person to really get a feel for it."

Andrew frowned. "You don't ever get to wander into the mountains without a conversation and verbal approval from your mother and I. A voicemail won't cut it." Smarty Pants cheeks blushed pink from disappointing his parents. Seeing that he was truly sorry in the rear view mirror, Andrew carried on with the previous response his son gave him. "What historical site did you think was up here? You didn't go into the mine, did you?"

"No! I was too scared," Fraidy Cat said quickly. It was the most honest thing he'd said all day.

"Good," Andrew said firmly. "You boys stay away from there. It's not a place for adventures. It's dangerous." Nods of agreement were seen through the mirror. "Are you sleeping over tonight, Freddy?" he asked, changing the subject.

"Actually," Smarty Pants said, thinking fast, "we were hoping to have the sleepover at Freddy's house again, Dad. Everything's already set up there, so you and Mom don't have to worry about us being too loud in the middle of the night." He and Fraidy Cat knew that if they let others in on the disappearance, that they might lose her forever. Seeing the watcher confirmed this. They had to protect her, at any cost.

Andrew hesitated, then nodded. "All right. Just behave. And don't keep his mom up all night."

After a quick stop for burgers, he dropped the boys off at Fraidy Cat's house. They waved goodbye and shut the door, finally breathing easy again.

By the time they climbed the stairs to Fraidy Cat's room, exhaustion had replaced fear. The boys collapsed onto their beds, barely getting under the covers before drifting into sleep.

Smarty Pants dreamt of the mine, of choosing between two tunnels that led nowhere, always getting lost. Fraidy Cat's dreams were worse. He kept seeing a pair of glowing eyes watching him from the dark.

Crash!

Both boys bolted upright. For a moment, neither spoke, unsure if they were still dreaming.

Smarty Pants jumped up, his ankle zinging, and grabbed the baseball bat by the bedroom door. Fraidy Cat snatched the flashlight from his backpack, the same one they'd carried into the mine earlier.

Heartbeats thudding, they crept downstairs. Smarty Pants wincing with each step on his tender ankle.

They reached the main floor and peered their heads around the wall. The entrance hallway was a mess. The decorative fruit bowl lay shattered across the floor, glass glittering under the beam of the flashlight; plastic berries and lemons still rolling. The phone cord swung slightly on its hook, like someone had brushed past it in a hurry.

And then they saw it.

The front door stood open.

As they navigated their bare feet around the broken glass, they eventually made their way to the front door, closing it tightly. With the dead bolt in place this time, they peered out the window behind the curtain. No one was there. Fraidy Cat noticed a crumbly feeling under his bare feet. Shining his flashlight to the floor, making sure it wasn't glass, he saw what the culprit was.

Speckles of dirt trailed in the hallway. On the entry rug below the door was a single, dirty shoe print.

Stamped into the mud of the shoe print was one word: *Bawden.*

8

The Squeak of Suspicion

As dawn broke, birds sang outside the window. But inside, the scene was far from peaceful. Furniture was stacked in front of the bedroom door, shoe rack, dresser, chair, anything not nailed down had been turned into a barricade. At the far end of the room sat a single bed, with a makeshift one of a foam pad and stacked blankets on the floor beside it. In those beds slept two boys who looked like they could use a week's rest.

"Who's there!" Fraidy Cat shot upright, eyes wide. He looked around in confusion before realizing he'd been dreaming. But when his gaze fell on the barricaded door, he sighed, his nightmare had followed him into real life.

Smarty Pants jolted awake at the noise. Still half-asleep, he grabbed the baseball bat and stood up, legs prickling with pins and needles. When he realized there was no danger, he relaxed, giving attention to his ankle that was still sore; the lack of peaceful rest slowing down his recovery. Smarty Pants exchanged a tired glance with Fraidy Cat. Both boys knew rest would have to wait.

They silently cleared the barricade, freeing the door. But neither wanted to open it. The memory of last night's watcher lingered.

Finally, Smarty Pants reached out, hand trembling as he gripped the cold doorknob. The hinges groaned as he cracked it open. Peering through the slit in the door, he checked for anyone lying in wait to attack them. Nothing. Just an empty hallway. He stepped out, bat in hand, Fraidy Cat close behind.

Smarty Pants hobbled a little as they crept down the stairs, careful to avoid the creaky spots, not wanting to alert an intruder of their location. To their relief, the front door was still locked tight, deadbolt in place.

After collecting up the broken glass and replacing the decorative fruit bowl with a plastic one from the kitchen, the boys gathered supplies, snacks, drinks, and the baseball bat, and retreated upstairs to the office.

Setting their loot down in the center of operations on the floor in the office, Smarty Pants limped over to the computer desk. Seeing his fearless friend in pain, Fraidy Cat left the office to gather different supplies. When he returned, Smarty Pants saw that Fraidy Cat was holding a bandage wrap, ice pack, and a small medicine bottle. After reading the instructions carefully and wrapping his ankle as best they could, they stacked up some books off the book shelf to prop his leg up while he sat at the computer, an ice pack draped over his injury.

Now that his injury was taken care of, Smarty Pants sat at the computer, determination on his face. He typed one word into the search bar, the word that had haunted his dreams: *Bawden.*

At first, the results were random, sports equipment brands, fast food names, law agencies, nothing that was actually helpful. Narrowing his search, Smarty Pants typed *Shoes* next to the word from the shoe print and an image of a leather shoe caught his eye. One click later, he was deep into the past.

Pine City Gazette, March 3, 1921:

Once a symbol of fine craftsmanship and luxury, the Bawden Shoe Company officially ceased operations this week after nearly two decades in business. Founded in 1903 by Henry Bawden, a prominent business man in Pine City, the company gained a reputation for its hand-stitched leather boots and dress shoes, often favored by miners and businessmen alike.

Financial troubles and growing tensions surrounding the closing of the Maple Hollow Mine have been cited as contributing factors in the company's sudden downfall. The Bawden family has since retreated from public life, leaving behind a legacy as polished as their shoes and a trail of unanswered questions about their final days in business.

"It's all connected," Fraidy Cat whispered. "The shoe, the mine, my great-great-grandpa... But how does my mom fit into this?" His voice cracked with worry. He knew that if they couldn't figure this out, he could lose his mom forever and end up an orphan.

"We'll find out," Smarty Pants said, his confidence steadying them both. "There's still a piece missing. We just have to figure out what it is." Frustration was building up inside Smarty. Usually he loved cracking codes, but he typically had all the information. Right now, he was feeling like he was given a puzzle that was a few pieces shy.

As Smarty Pants scanned the room for ideas, desperate for a direction to continue the search, sunlight slipped through the window and landed on their center of operations. There it was, next to a soda can, the journal from Edwin Carver that so far held more mysteries than answers.

Maybe that is where the pieces are, inside the journal that kept its secrets hidden in a riddle. He started toward it, ankle already feeling better and ready to dive back into Edwin's clues, but before he could reach it...

Bang! Bang! Bang!

The sound echoed from downstairs.

Fraidy Cat nearly jumped out of his skin, flailing his arms around and knocking over his water bottle. Smarty Pants placed his finger to his mouth, motioning his friend to be quiet. They crept to the window that overlooked the front porch and peered down. Standing there, holding a small white envelope, was neighborly Mr. Kadburgler.

Curious, the boys hurried down stairs. Trying to slow their breath, trying not to alarm Mr. Kadburgler, they paused for a moment to breathe.

Bang! Bang! Bang!

"Coming!" Fraidy Cat blurted instinctively before realizing how much his voice trembled. Taking the lead, Smarty Pants sensed his friend was still nervous and opened the door just enough to see the visitor, Fraidy Cat peering out with him, but staying behind his friend.

"I got your mother's mail by accident," said Mr. Kadburgler, his mustache twitching, teeth slightly exposed, resembling a rat. He held out an envelope, daring Fraidy Cat to come out from behind his friend and take it from him.

"Oh... thanks..." Fraidy Cat said, reaching around Smarty Pants for the envelope, hoping within it was a clue. As he motioned to pull the envelope closer to him, Mr. Kadburgler didn't let go. Rather, he stared straight into Fraidy's eyes. The envelope started shaking under Fraidy's trembling hand.

"You seem scared. Is everything alright?" His voice was soft, too soft. Concern feeling forced rather than genuine.

To Smarty Pants, the moment felt like a cat toying with a mouse. Not wanting to see his friend becoming prey, he snatched the envelope from Mr. Kadburgler's hand, reclaiming the power between them. "We're fine," he said firmly. "We're working on our school project." Smarty Pants tucked the envelope in his rear jean pocket.

The three stood there in silence. Smarty Pants could feel Kadburgler's gaze shift past them, peering into the house, analyzing its condition. Smarty pushed the door slightly more shut.

Kadburgler sighed. "Well, tell your mother I stopped by if you see her," he said, turning toward the steps heading down.

Squeak. Squeak. Squeak.

Each step of his fancy leather shoes made a sharp sound. Smarty Pants' eyes followed them. Mud-caked shoes. Polished leather. Luxury brand. Old design. Bawden.

His stomach twisted. Those weren't just shoes.

They were a clue walking away, and within them, their suspect.

9

The Bloodline

With the door closed, the boys stood there, staring at each other. The realization of Mr. Kadburgler being the watcher in the woods was overwhelming. Yes, he had been suspicious, but it felt more real actually knowing it was the person that lived closest to Fraidy Cat. The person that he would help bring groceries into his house. It felt too real. Fraidy Cat was shaken from the encounter with his "friendly neighbor", but Smarty Pants was buzzing with determination. He knew who the watcher was. Now, he was going to catch him in the act.

Smarty Pants bolted upstairs, only slightly limping, eager to resume the investigation, excited to add this puzzle piece. Although he didn't like the idea that Fraidy Cat's mom could be in danger, he couldn't deny how much he loved detective work. It was like being inside one of his favorite books, except this time, *he* got to make the choices.

Out of breath from racing up the flight of stairs in three swift motions, Smarty reached the office doorway, grasping it for balance. He welcomed the smell of dust and leather, excited to continue his investigation. As he hopped up onto the leather office chair and rested his hands on the desk, Fraidy Cat had finally entered the room, exhausted from trying to keep up with Smarty Pants. Across the room, at the computer, Smarty Pants typed another word beside Bawden: *Kadburgler.*

Not much came up—both were very unique names. However, one line of information formed on the screen that made both boys freeze:

The marriage of Henry Bawden's daughter, Elizabeth, to Greggory Kadburgler.

That meant that Mr. Kadburgler's grandpa had married Henry Bawden's daughter. Henry Bawden was the owner of the shoe company. The very shoe company that was around during the mining days of Maple Hollow mine. It was their smoking gun. The connection between the shoe company, the mine, and Mr. Kadburgler. All the pieces of the puzzle were finally starting to fit together. Smarty Pants now had a connection for his suspect to the mystery. All that was left was determining the motive for Mrs. Carver's disappearance. Was she hiding or was she taken?

"Why?" Fraidy Cat managed to whisper, wondering what the motive could be too. His voice cracked with fear and confusion.

Smarty Pants turned to answer, but the sight of tears swelling in his friend's eyes stopped him. Fraidy felt raw. He felt as though everyone knew the inside joke and was laughing at him. He wanted to know why this was all happening. He wanted his mom back, she was all he had left. Years ago, Mr. Carver, the firefighter hero, risked his life in a fire to save the people inside. He saved them, but he paid the price. Fraidy Cat felt the pain of his dad being gone every day. He didn't want his mom to be gone too.

"Why would Mr. Kadburgler want my mom? Why would he want to hurt us? What did we ever do to him?" Fraidy Cat dropped to the floor, shoulders shaking. The fear, the sleepless nights, the shock, it all broke loose at once.

Smarty Pants sat beside him and pulled him into a quick, awkward hug. He didn't have the answers, but he wasn't going to let his friend face it alone.

Fraidy Cat allowed the tears to stream down his face, finally facing all the hurt he had bottled up. Through sobbing and panting, he kept muttering "why?" as he let himself feel all the emotions he tucked away. After a few minutes, the tears slowed. As his breathing returned to normal, Fraidy Cat rubbed his eyes, and Smarty Pants gave his back a reassuring pat.

"There has to be more to this," Smarty Pants said quietly. Mind racing. The pieces just weren't fitting. He wanted nothing more than to slam them together and make them fit, but he knew that wouldn't help anyone.

He kept thinking, trying to figure out how Fraidy's mom fit into the story.

"Bawden was around during the mine days, that article even

mentioned it. What if Henry Bawden was connected to the mine too?"

Fraidy Cat looked up, grateful for the distraction from worrying about his mom. "You think Bawden also owned the mine?"

"It would fit, wouldn't it? A rich family in a small town, they probably owned more than one business. If the Bawden's owned the mine, that means Mr. Kadburgler is tied to it too. He would have been the heir of the mine if it never went bankrupt since his grandpa married Henry Bawden's daughter."

"Then... his family *stole* the diamond?" Fraidy Cat asked. He too was trying to finish the puzzle.

Smarty Pants shook his head. That wouldn't make sense. If Mr. Kadburgler's family stole the Mother Diamond, why would he be threatening Fraidy's mom? What would he stand to win?

Silence hung heavy between them. Smarty Pants leaned back in the chair, turning the idea over in his mind. It made sense... almost. He just couldn't come up with any reason as to how Mrs. Carver was involved in this?

He sighed and slumped into the chair. The sound of crinkling paper from underneath Smarty Pants broke the quiet.

He sat up, curiosity driving this current investigation. As he got to his feet, he looked around for the source of the sound. There was nothing on the worn leather seat that would have made the noise. Smarty Pants started to pat his body, trying to find the source of the noise. When he patted his rear jean pocket, the crinkling paper noise rang out again. Hand reaching inside his pocket, he pulled out a single white envelope, creased and wrinkled. It was the envelope that Mr. Kadburgler had brought over to them.

Smarty Pants looked it over. A postage stamp was absent from it, as well as a return address. The only writing that adorned the envelope was big, uneven letters across the front that read:

Merilyn Carver.

Trembling, Smarty Pants' eyes widened, causing alarm. Fraidy Cat rushed to his friend's side, when he saw the envelope his heart nearly stopped. "That's my mom." He abruptly ripped the envelope out of Smarty's hands and tore it open. Inside was one single sheet of paper, folded neatly in half.

He unfolded it, hands shaking, heart racing and read the message written in red ink:

If you don't bring me the diamond, it won't be the only mother that goes missing!

10

The Right Choice

Silence sat heavy in the dusty office. The only sound was the soft crinkle of paper in Fraidy Cat's quaking hands. This was the proof he had been dreading. The proof that someone was targeting his mom, out to get her. Gone were the hopeful thoughts of his mom hiding out somewhere safe. She was being threatened. Someone was intentionally trying to hurt her. Now all he could picture was her tied up, trapped, and terrified.

Smarty Pants' brain raced through every possibility, desperate to find something, anything, to reassure his friend. But the words in red ink said it all: *it won't be the only mother that goes missing.* Someone *was* threatening her and now she was gone.

Then, like spotting a needle in a haystack, a flicker of hope crossed his mind.

"Wait," Smarty said quickly. "How did this envelope end up in Mr. Kadburgler's mailbox by accident?" He said this last word with sarcasm, giving this unbelievable story air quotes. Then he thought harder, more seriously. "We know Mr. Kadburgler is the watcher. But maybe the person threatening your mom is someone different. If it was Mr. Kadburgler, then he would know that your mom isn't here right now. He would know she would never read that letter. So maybe they are two different people. Why else would she still be getting threatening letters?"

Fraidy Cat looked up, the panic in his eyes dimming for a second.

"You're right..." he said with a shaky sigh. The whole room seemed to exhale with him.

"She could still be okay. Maybe she's hiding."

"I really hope you're right, but this feels like a trap." Fraidy said quietly. "Also, wouldn't she try to call me if she was just hiding? Check in?"

Smarty thought hard. That was true. She would have. Then it hit him.

"She *did* contact us," he said, eyes lighting up. "That creepy phone call warning us to not trust anyone the first night. That had to be her! And I bet she meant Mr. Kadburgler specifically."

Fraidy frowned, replaying the call in his mind. The voice hadn't quite sounded like his mom... but it had *felt* like her somehow. Familiar. Safe.

"I think you might be right," he said softly, not wanting to let hope hurt him again. "But why nothing since then?"

"I don't know. But maybe if we solve this mystery, find out who's threatening her then she'll come home." Smarty's voice steadied. "One step at a time."

"One step at a time. Okay," Fraidy said, nodding in agreement. "So where do we start?"

This question had been on Smarty's mind since the first note that they had found in the sandwich. He didn't want to admit that he didn't know where to go next. He felt like he was constantly falling into the next move. He scanned the room, looking for a clue to point him in the right direction. He remembered! Smarty's eyes drifted toward the open journal on the desk again. The final page lying open, waiting for someone to crack the ancient code.

"We start here." Reaching for the journal, Smarty grabbed it and walked over to the center of operations, trying to get comfortable on the floor.

The boys sat down side by side, digging back into the coded message. They were so focused they didn't even stop for snacks, ignoring the desperate cries coming from their stomachs.

Journal open, Smarty traced the lines of the riddle with his finger, muttering.

When the light glows blue, choose one or two.

His mind was running through as many different options he could think of that included a blue light, however, he kept coming up empty. Then an image of a blue glow occupied his brain.

"That's it," he said. "We already found where the light glows blue! The mineral walls in the mine. And remember? It forked into two tunnels. We just didn't know which one to pick."

Fraidy Cat's shoulders sank, he was hoping this would lead them anywhere but that dangerous mine. "But how do we *know* which one?" Fraidy's voice wavered. "The wrong way could be... fatal."

Smarty paced the room, repeating the line under his breath. "Choose one or two... choose one or two..."

He paced that path so many times he was wearing down the shaggy carpet and causing his ankle to flare up in pain again.

Then Fraidy cracked an exhausted joke. "Yeah, well, if we *choose right,* it'll be our *last night*" motioning a slicing hand across his neck, quickly followed by his tongue falling out and closing his eyes.

Smarty froze mid-step, his eyes widening. "That's it!"

"What's it? I don't want it to be my last night!"

"The answer. It's *left!* The message says *choose one or two,* but if you choose 'right,' it'll be your last night. The right tunnel leads to danger. We have to go left!" Smarty collapsed into the nearby leather chair, spinning it in victory, giving his ankle a break.

"So we take the left tunnel, that's simple enough," Fraidy said slowly, "but then there's that part about the gate. *'When you approach the gate, give it the answer to learn your fate.'* What's the answer? What's the question?"

Smarty leaned back, exhausted. "I don't know yet. There's still something we're missing." He read that riddle so many times he could recite it by heart, but there were no questions in it, no answers to find. Maybe the question is in the mine.

Then he looked up at Fraidy, offering a half-grin that meant trouble.

Fraidy read his mind immediately. "No. I'm not going back to that creepy mine."

Smarty smirked. "You got a better plan?"

"Yes. Stay home forever." He nestled down into their center of operations, snuggling a pillow close to his chest.

"Come on, Fraidy. We've got to go back. If we don't, we'll never find your mom."

Fraidy groaned, he would do anything for his mom. He supposed anything did mean facing certain death in the mine. "We don't even have our bikes anymore. How are we supposed to get there?"

Smarty shrugged. "We could ask Mr. Kadburgler for a ride." A teasing smile was draped across his face.

Fraidy's jaw dropped. "You're insane. I'll go into that creepy mine again, but I draw the line at Mr. Kadburgler!"

"Okay, okay," Smarty said, laughing. "We'll take the old scooters."

"I hate that idea too," Fraidy said, knowing that they were housed in the shed out back, "but fine. You're killing all the spiders we find though."

As they approached the shed, Fraidy sent Smarty in first. The last time Fraidy entered the old shed, he was with his mom, and a large spider landed on his head. This time, he came prepared, bug spray in one hand, fly swatter in the other.

Two spider attacks later, the boys were packing their backpacks, hoping for the best, but preparing for the worst. They knew that soon, they would be returning to the mine.

Inside that mine, they knew a question was waiting.

They just hoped they'd have the answer.

11

The Shadow

As they stepped outside the front door with scooters in hand, a sound like soft rain filled the air, but when Fraidy Cat looked up, the sky was bone dry. Curious, the boys followed the sound until they found the source.

Next door, Mr. Kadburgler stood on his front lawn, watering his prized possessions, his petunias. They were everywhere: hanging from the porch, lining the walkway, filling the flowerbeds in neat rainbow rows. Not a single petal drooped, not one leaf dared turn brown. His lawn looked more like a painting than a yard, every shrub trimmed to perfection, every blade of grass standing at attention.

But something was off. Near the corner of the yard, Mr. Kadburgler kept watering the same patch of flowers long after it had turned to mud. That was strange enough, but to make things worse, his gaze wasn't on the flowers at all—it was fixed on Fraidy Cat's house. More specifically, his mom's office window.

The slam of Fraidy's front door snapped him out of his trance. His head jerked down, eyes locking squarely onto Fraidy Cat.

Shrinking under that icy stare, Fraidy hurried down the steps with his scooter, wishing he could melt into the pavement. Smarty Pants followed close behind, balancing on his rusted scooter beside him, challenging Mr. Kadburgler's gaze.

"I hate that he stares at me like that," Fraidy Cat whispered, his voice barely audible. "Like I'm being hunted."

"Stare back at him. Prove to him that he has no power over you. Stand tall." To prove his point, and never one to back down, Smarty Pants stared right back. He didn't blink. Didn't move. Just stared.

Then something shifted.

Movement.

Inside the Kadburgler house. Up high in the attic window in the center of a peak high on the house, the first story roof just below it. The window was decorated in detailed trim that resembled a gingerbread house. The glass pane frosted, but larger than a usual attic window.

It was common knowledge that Mr. Kadburgler lived alone, not even a pet to keep him company. However, he was outside, leaving the boys to speculate on who, or what, could be dwelling in Fraidy's creepy neighbor's house.

Smarty squinted, hoping to catch some type of identifying detail from the shadow. "Wait... who's in there?"

The movement again came from Mr. Kadburgler's attic window. The movement turned into a shadow; the shadow turned into the silhouette of a person. They were still and watching. They had been so still that the boys thought their minds were playing a trick on them and that it wasn't alive at all. Ready to shrug the movement in the attic off, their eyes lingered for a half second longer.

Then *bang!*

A hand slammed against the glass.

Both boys jumped.

Another hit. And another. The shadow was pounding the window now, frantic, desperate. Then, as suddenly as it started, it stopped.

The shadow vanished.

The attic window returned to silence.

Slowly, the boys' eyes lowered from the window and met Mr. Kadburgler's again. He hadn't moved an inch, other than one hand that was now tucked inside his jacket pocket. The other remained holding the hose as it continued to pour water onto the same flooded patch of ground.

Trying to act casual, Fraidy gave a weak wave, a silent way of saying *Oops, I caught you staring.*

Mr. Kadburgler didn't wave back. He was not embarrassed for staring, he was being intentional. It seemed he wanted them to know he was watching them. He wanted them to feel his eyes burning into their skin. His eyes followed them all the way down the street, unblinking.

When they finally turned the corner, Fraidy exhaled the breath he'd been holding.

"First the mine, now Mr. Kadburgler's house is haunted too!" he said, gripping his handlebars so tightly his knuckles went white. "Do you think it's contagious? Is my house next?" his voice cracked in worry.

Smarty laughed nervously under his breath. "It's not haunted. Someone was *in there.*"

"Someone? Why would someone go into Mr. Kadburgler's house? He is crazy!" Fraidy retorted, eyes wide. "You think he's got a partner?" he speculated.

"Maybe," Smarty said thoughtfully. "Whoever it was seemed desperate to get his attention."

"Well, they can keep it. I wish I'd never have to see him again. Better yet, I wish he would never look at me again. His beady eyes give me goosebumps!"

Smarty chuckled again, giving a nod toward the road. "Come on. Let's keep moving. We don't want to be caught out here in the dark again."

Fraidy Cat jetted forward as fast as he could at this notion. He desperately did not want to go into the mine, but he refused to be in it after dark. He was hoping that since they left his house around noon, that they would make it back home before the sun set.

Their scooters weren't as fast as their bikes, but they were faster than walking, and less noisy than running. As they coasted toward the mine, Fraidy couldn't shake the memory of the shadow in the attic. Why would they have banged on the window? Didn't the noise give them away, exposing that Mr. Kadburgler had a secret partner? Something just didn't seem right about it.

Lost in thought, Fraidy didn't see the jagged mine entrance slowly come into view, but when he finally saw it, his stomach twisted. The last time they were here, their bikes had disappeared and they were abandoned all alone... with the watcher, no, with Mr. Kadburgler.

Smarty, noticing his friend's silent fear, dug through his backpack. "Don't worry. I came prepared."

The sound of metal hitting metal echoed in the open air. Smarty pulled out of his backpack a chain and a small padlock.

"Let's see someone try to steal our rides this time." Smarty wrapped the scooters together and secured them around a thick tree trunk. After checking his handiwork and determining the scooters were safe, he took a step back from the tree feeling a sense of pride.

Fraidy smiled. It wasn't much, but it helped to know Smarty thought of everything and that their scooters would be waiting for them when they emerged from the earth. Their eyes met giving each other an encouraging nod, then they turned toward the mine.

To Smarty Pants, the mine entrance held the answer to every mystery they'd been chasing. He was eager to finish this puzzle with the pieces Maple Hollow Mine was harboring.

To Fraidy Cat, the entrance looked like the mouth of a beast waiting to swallow them whole.

Before entering, they slipped on their headlamps, took a deep breath, and then slowly crept inside.

The air was cool, thick with dust and mystery. Somewhere deep within, the mine groaned. Wood settling, rocks shifting, earth whispering warnings.

The world here had long forgotten people. It preferred silence.

But not today.

Today, its secrets would be revealed.

12

The Left Path

Smarty Pants led the way through the mine, his headlamp beam guiding them forward. The color brown coated everything inside: the rocks, the dirt, the bugs. Wind drifted through the tunnel, breathing life into the darkness. The smell of damp dirt sticking to their skin as it wafted through the air. As insects and unseen creatures stirred from their unwelcome visitors, Fraidy Cat clung to his friend's backpack, making sure he wasn't left behind.

What felt like endless darkness finally began to shift. Ahead, the familiar faint blue glow shimmered in the distance. Step by step, it grew brighter until it illuminated the tunnel walls, leaving their headlamps useless.

Fraidy Cat, unaware that his fearless leader had stopped, ran straight into the backpack that had been his lifeline.

"Sorry," Fraidy Cat groaned, rubbing his forehead and looking to see what had caused his friend to abruptly stop.

Smarty Pants was staring ahead of him, not even noticing the collision he was just involved in. Before him stood a choice; a choice that would decide their fate.

Two paths stretched out before them, each identical, each equally foreboding.

If you choose right, it will be your last night.

The warning echoed in both boys' minds.

Smarty Pants confidently lifted his foot, aiming towards the left path. Fraidy seized Smarty's arm, stopping him before he could step.

"What if we're wrong?" Fraidy Cat was visibly trembling, body quaking.

"We aren't. I'm certain of it." Smarty rested his foot where it previously came from. "Do you trust me?"

"Yes." Fraidy Cat whispered without thought. He trusted Smarty Pants explicitly.

With a nod of understanding, Smarty Pants hesitantly lifted his foot again and stepped down the left path with Fraidy Cat following close behind.

As they walked, Fraidy Cat was waiting for their doom to come. For the floor to fall out from under them or the ceiling to fall in on them. He trusted Smarty Pants, but he doubted himself.

On the other hand, Smarty Pants felt certain they chose the correct path. He was searching for anything that could resemble a gate: a pile of sticks, a strange rock formation, even a shadow that might pass as one.

He was beginning to give up hope, doubt settling in. Suddenly, the familiar crunch of dirt beneath their shoes changed. The ground felt harder, solid... metallic.

Smack!

Fraidy Cat tripped and tumbled forward into his friend's back-pack once again, sending both boys crashing to the ground in a heap of groans and echoes. The ceiling of the mine began to grumble, awakening from noise. The boys froze, even slowing their breathing to remain as quiet as possible.

Once the ceiling had rested, they slowly began returning to their feet. Smarty Pants winced, his ankle stinging with pain again after the fall. As he bent down to rub the sore spot on his ankle, he began examining the floor. He found a gleaming track running beneath the dust.

"Mine cart tracks," he whispered, his voice tinged with excite-ment, trying to mask his pain.

The rusted rails stretched deep into the tunnel, vanishing into darkness. Once, these tracks carried precious stones from the earth's belly; now they were just ghosts of the past, leading the boys deeper into the mine.

To Smarty Pants, the tracks were a symbol of a good omen, that trusting his instincts and following the riddle were the right choice. However, to Fraidy Cat, they were more tripping hazards.

They followed the tracks until the tunnel widened into a cavern. Heavy rocks and beams lined the walls and ceilings. Rubble and leftover tools, pick axes, hard hats, and leather bags lined the floor, relics of the past.

Blocking their path stood a massive, iron gate that reached from floor to ceiling. Its bars were thick, rusted, and tangled with cobwebs.

"This is it," Smarty Pants breathed. "We picked the right path!" Quiet celebration replacing his doubt.

For once, both boys shared the same feeling: relief.

Smarty was relieved that the mystery was unfolding, while Fraidy was relieved that they hadn't died.

They each pushed against the gate, but it wouldn't budge. When they tried again, a small shower of dirt sprinkled from the ceiling.

They stopped immediately.

One wrong move and the whole cavern could come down on them.

"What do we do now?" Fraidy Cat's voice cracked. "The gate's locked, there's no question to answer, and we're trapped. How are we going to get my mom back now?"

Smarty Pants paused, thinking carefully, his mind returning to the riddle. "We need to look around for the question. There has to be something here. The gate is not going to open by force."

The two began searching the cavern for any sign of a clue. They turned over rocks, brushed the walls, and examined every old tool left behind by the miners. They even were trying the tools on the gate, both in the lock and at the hinge, but they all failed, the path remaining blocked.

Defeated, Fraidy Cat slumped to the ground. His shoulders sagged and his eyes closed. "We came all this way... for nothing."

He felt hollow. After losing his dad, his mom was all he had left, and now he was losing her too.

Smarty Pants kept scanning the cavern, desperate for anything to pull his friend out of despair. Then, something caught his eye, hanging from the ceiling near the gate, locked in the room with them.

A bird cage.

"Do you know why miners used to keep birds down here?" Smarty asked, excited to answer his own question and hopeful to pull Fraidy from his despair.

Fraidy Cat blinked and glanced up. "Birds? In a mine?"

"Canaries," Smarty explained. "Miners used them to detect dangerous gases. If the canary got weak or fell off its perch, it meant poison in the air."

Fraidy Cat flinched at the word poison, he was already worried about a cave-in, now he had to add poisonous gases to the list. But curiosity drew him out of his lurch, picking himself up off the floor. He stepped beside his friend, peering up at the cage.

When Fraidy peered into the cage, his extra two inches of height allowed him to see the contents of the bird cage. Inside, glinting faintly in the glow of his headlamp, was a large iron key, its bronze coating dulled with age and dust.

"Smarty," Fraidy whispered, "it's here. It's the key for the gate."

"What!" Smarty whispered in excitement. "Get it! Let's try it and see if it works." He was on his tip toes, trying hard to see what was out of his line of sight.

Fraidy Cat reached for the bird cage door, but when he reached up to open it, the small door wouldn't budge. It was locked.

"Of course it's locked," Fraidy groaned. "Everything down here is locked. Why are we always in need of a key?"

Then it hit him. He had a key. The one hanging around his neck since the first night his mother disappeared. The small key they found in the box buried in his backyard that his mom warned him to keep safe. The same key that once hung around his dad's neck and was pictured in Edwin's journal.

Heart pounding, Fraidy Cat slipped the chain off from around his head. The metal brushed against his skin, cold and heavy, like it knew the weight of what was coming.

He stepped closer, lifted his trembling hand, and placed the key into the birdcage lock.

He hesitated, looked back at Smarty Pants, then slowly began to turn the key.

13

The Weight of Secrets

Click!

The sweet sound of the bird cage lock opening echoed through the cavern. Fraidy Cat inhaled deeply, savoring the moment. Finally, something was going right. When he exhaled, he knew it was time to move forward and face the next part of the mystery. But how would the next clue reveal itself?

The gate to the bird cage creaked open. He reached into the cage, his fingers brushing against cold metal. As he pulled the old key free, the rust crumbled beneath his grip like dry earth.

Once in the light of their headlamps, the key seemed to mirror the old iron gate blocking their path: ancient, heavy, and holding a secret that wanted to be revealed.

Fraidy Cat slid the large key into the large gate's lock. The gears groaned in protest, stiff with age. He twisted, but it wouldn't budge.

Smarty Pants placed his hands over Fraidy's, lending his strength. Together, they turned. The lock screeched in resistance — then gave way. It had probably been decades since anyone had used it.

Creeeaaakkk!

The massive gate shuddered open, stirring a storm of dust that swirled around their heads. When the air settled, so did the boys' excitement. They both sensed it. Once they crossed that threshold, there would be no turning back.

"It's going to be okay," Smarty Pants said, his voice trembling between excitement and fear.

Fraidy Cat gnawed at his lip. *You're going to chew a hole straight through*, he could almost hear his mom say. The thought made him grin. If she could see him now, his lip would be the least of her worries.

Mom. I have to do this for Mom.

In a rare burst of courage, Fraidy Cat stepped forward first. Smarty Pants grinned, proud to see his friend leading the way.

"So, what do you think we are supposed to be looking for now?" Fraidy Cat said as he was scanning the new tunnel they were in.

"I don't know," Smarty Pants sighed. He couldn't shake the feeling that they still didn't give the answer that was mentioned in the riddle. *When you approach the gate, give it the answer to learn your fate.* They found a gate. They went through the gate. But what answer did they give? It just wasn't adding up. It felt incomplete. "Just keep your eyes peeled for anything that looks out of the ordinary."

They continued down the new tunnel before seeing something that made them stop. Just like earlier in the tunnels, a faint blue glow shimmered on the floor near a wall up ahead, a rock, pulsing like a heartbeat in the dark.

They hadn't seen any blue glowing stones since the path that forked.

As they approached the faint blue glow that was emitting from a rock on the floor, they realized the glow wasn't random. Someone had carved into the surface, exposing veins of the shining mineral beneath. Smarty Pants crouched down and traced the etching of his find with his finger: a single line down the middle of the front of the rock with three small circles on either side of it. As his finger continued to draw the etching's path, he realized the circles on the rock reminded him of the circles on a dice.

"I think we should hold on to this. It might be a clue," he said. *It might be the answer*, he thought.

Fraidy Cat nodded. Smarty gently pried the grapefruit-sized rock from the floor, clutching it carefully.

A few yards farther, another glowing rock appeared. This one bore a new symbol: one line down the middle with two circles on one side of the line and four on the other. Fraidy Cat took it, sharing the load.

Two more times this happened; each stone etched with a unique design of a line down the middle with a number of circles on either side of it. By the time they reached the fifth glowing rock, their arms were full and ached under their weight.

"What are we going to do?" Fraidy Cat panted. "My arms are tired. I can't carry any more without dropping them."

The added weight Smarty Pants was carrying was putting pressure on his already swollen ankle. He was also desperate to be relieved of the rocks. Smarty Pants looked around then spotted the solution up ahead. An old mine cart sat rusting on the tracks.

"Let's do like your ancestors," he said with a grin, moving toward the cart. They quickly unloaded their rocks into the cart. Fraidy sighed in relief as the weight left his arms, feeling the blood rush through them.

They pushed the cart forward on the tracks, collecting ten more glowing stones, each carved with its own unique number of circles. Then, suddenly, the tracks ended. The tunnel ahead had disappeared, a wall of dirt and stone closing off the path. The site of a cave-in from the past.

Fraidy Cat inhaled the thick scent of wet earth. Smarty stood beside him, scanning the collapse, his ankle screaming for rest, but his mind racing for a solution. But this time, there wasn't one. They'd hit a dead end, literally.

Fraidy Cat leaned against the rock wall, hands rubbing on his thighs, breath quivering. "There is no more riddle left to follow. We chose the path. We unlocked the gate. Is this our fate? Being buried alive in the depths of the earth?" Fraidy Cat had reached the point of delirium.

"That can't be it. This can't be the end. There has to be something more." It was Smarty Pants' turn to wallow in self doubt. He was second guessing every choice he had made. What if he had led them down the wrong path? What if he was the cause of their doom? But one thought kept racing through his mind. What was the answer they were supposed to give?

"Look! Another bird cage!" Fraidy Cat pointed to one hanging on the right side of the track.

"There's one over here too," Smarty said, spotting another on the left. "Why put two cages so close together?"

The question gnawed at him. He stepped closer to the one on the left. When he reached it, he perched himself up on a rock, trying to see if there were any contents inside. When he saw it was empty, he returned to his normal height, resting his heels back on the rock, his ankle throbbing. The rock shifted beneath his feet. Smarty Pants tumbled to protect his already injured ankle, knocking the bird cage with an arm reaching out trying to catch his fall. As the bird cage swung from its fixture on the ceiling, Smarty Pants saw an etching under the bird cage. "There's a number under this cage!"

Fraidy rushed to check the cage on the right. "This one too!"

"This has to be part of it," Smarty breathed. "The bird cages are part of the riddle."

"But what do the numbers mean?" Fraidy's voice wavered with exhaustion.

It all seemed random, the etchings on the rocks, the numbers under the cage. How did these all connect? What could these numbers mean?

Smarty Pants paced the small distance between the bird cages, attempting to walk off the pain of his ankle. He was trying to think of the solution, but his mind kept coming up blank. He paced over to the cart that was illuminated by a blue glow. Smarty picked up a rock on top, tracing the etching again. This rock had the same line down the middle of it with two circles on each side of it. An idea finally sparked! Smarty Pants frantically looked over each stone they had collected. Circles. Each stone had circles.

Smarty thought back to the next part of the riddle: *When you reach the gate, give it the answer to learn your fate.*

Smarty leaned closer, eyes widening. "That's it! The circles on the rocks must add up to the numbers on the cages. We have to give each cage the right answer!"

Smarty Pants took this rock over to the left bird cage and placed it inside. As he let go of the rock, the bird cage shifted lower under the weight, while the right bird cage shifted higher.

"Each of these rocks must have a different weight. We need to get them the answer of the correct weight. I bet these circles also add up to the number under each cage."

They got to work organizing the rocks on the floor from smallest to largest in the number of circles etched into them. It was grueling. They were lifting, balancing, and swapping stones. Their hands blistered and bled as they tried to get the correct answer, the cages shifting like uneven scales.

Finally, as the last rock slid into place, the cages moved one last time. The right bird cage was slightly taller than the left. Fraidy Cat and Smarty Pants took a step back and waited.

But nothing happened.

The only sound was their heavy breathing and the faint squeaks of creatures stirring in the darkness.

Then a low, grinding rumble rose behind them.

The earth trembled. Dust rained from the ceiling. Fraidy turned just in time to see the wall behind him shifting. It was alive and moving.

The secret that had lain dormant all these years was about to be revealed.

14

The Heart of the Mine

A grumbling wall of rocks near one of the bird cages began to shift, revealing a hidden passageway. As the dust settled around the boys, a faint glow came into focus. The tunnel shimmered with an eerie blue light. As the blue glow melted up their faces, they remained in stunned silence.

This secret entrance was the reward for solving the riddle written in a journal many years ago. They had worked so hard to achieve this success. Now that it was in front of them, they hesitated to cross the finish line.

Smarty Pants was feeling accomplished, he had really solved the riddle, but he felt a little saddened by the thought of it all being over. He wanted to find Fraidy's mom, but he also wasn't ready to hang up his detective hat.

Fraidy Cat inhaled deeply and thought of his mom, picturing her at home, waiting for him. Then he thought of Edwin Carver, the legacy that he created. He wanted to honor him and make him proud. This desire moved him forward, walking toward the blue lights; Smarty Pants following his lead.

When they stepped inside, enveloped by the blue glow, their eyes widened. Every inch of the walls was covered in exposed fluorite, the same mineral from the glowing blue lights and the etched stones. The cool air in the glowing room sent a shiver down their spine, making them curl their toes. The damp dirt air was replaced with the smell of stale rocks. The air buzzed faintly, and the boys felt as though they had stepped into another world. After hours surrounded by the dark, suffocating mine, the sudden brilliance of the room swallowed them up.

For a long moment, neither spoke. Then, cutting through the silence, Smarty Pants began to chuckle. He couldn't believe it; where they were, what they had done. Just a few days ago, they were kids who spent their afternoons playing video games and riding bikes. Now they were explorers who had solved a mystery buried for over a century.

He laughed harder, proud that his brain had actually beaten a challenge this big.

At first, Fraidy Cat flinched at the unexpected sound. After everything they'd faced, laughter felt out of place. But then, slowly, it bubbled out of him too. Relief washed over him. He felt like they were close, closer than ever, to finding his mom. Maybe soon, he'd finally get that hug he'd been missing.

Their soft chuckles grew into uncontrollable belly laughs, echoing through the glowing cavern.

And then they stopped. Abruptly.

In the center of the room, almost camouflaged by the blue glow, stood a small pedestal.

Cautiously, they approached, afraid to disturb whatever secret had slept there for decades. Resting atop the pedestal was a diamond; a massive one, unlike anything they had ever seen. The boys stared, their reflections glimmering on its surface.

Smarty Pants reached toward it, his fingertips hovering just inches away. Even from that distance, he could feel the static hum of energy pulsing off the stone, like a spark waiting to jump.

"It's been here all this time?" Fraidy Cat whispered. Smarty Pants was also confused by this revelation. "Why would the thieves bring it back? If I stole something this valuable, I'd sell it, not hide it away."

Smarty Pants was still trying to process everything. "The Mother has come home..." Smarty Pants murmured. The pieces were finally falling into place. "This is where it was found. The mine. It's her home. Elias and Edwin brought the Mother Diamond back. They returned her."

"Elias and Edwin are the thieves? They stole the Mother Diamond from the museum?" Fraidy Cat couldn't believe this accusation.

"It makes sense. This is the only place she was safe from those that intended to sell her, profit off of her. Edwin and Elias were the protectors. They were trying to save the Mother Diamond from being selfishly locked away. It's the only thing that makes sense."

"So you're saying Edwin and Elias stole the Mother Diamond from the museum and hid it away here? But if they were the thieves," Fraidy Cat said, his voice trembling, "then who's been sending my mom those letters? And where is she?"

Smarty Pants frowned. "You're right. It doesn't add up…"

Silence filled the room again. One boy thought of history and discovery; the other thought only of his mother.

"It has to be whoever sent the initial threat of robbery at the museum," Smarty Pants blurted. "The one that believes he is entitled to the Mother Diamond. The note said they were going to return for what is rightfully theirs."

Before Fraidy Cat could respond, Smarty Pants pressed his palm against the diamond. Energy surged through him. It was alive, electric. Without thinking, he lifted it from the pedestal.

Click!

The weight of the Mother Diamond being removed from the pedestal set off a trap. The walls began to grumble. The earth began to shake. The glowing blue light flickered and pulsed as shards rained from above. Fraidy Cat's stomach dropped. This was it, they were going to be trapped forever.

Panic surged. Fraidy scanned the collapsing chamber for any escape, desperate to survive. That's when he saw it, something out of place. A folded, yellowed piece of paper lying on the pedestal where the diamond had rested.

"Over here!" Smarty Pants shouted. He had spotted a narrow opening on the far wall. He grabbed Fraidy's arm, pulling him toward safety.

But Fraidy hesitated just long enough to snatch the note from the pedestal. *Maybe the answers are in here*, he thought desperately. *Maybe Mom's name is on it.*

Running to the opening, rocks began falling all around them, gradually getting larger. They were dodging and weaving boulders that fell overhead. Noticing an exceptionally large rock above the opening shaking, they moved faster, desperate for survival.

They squeezed through the narrow gap, Fraidy's backpack scraping against a rock, holding him back from reaching safety. He tugged and pulled frantically, but it would not release. Smarty Pants grabbed Fraidy Cat's hand as they both pulled together, dislodging Fraidy Cat and his backpack from the tunnel and pulling him safely into a side chamber. The boys laid on the floor huffing and panting.

Boom!

A rush of air blasted through the opening as the massive boulder crashed down, sealing the passage shut. Dust clouded around them. The boys coughed, hearts pounding, as silence returned.

They were alive but trapped.

Now, they had to find another way out before the mine became their tomb.

15

The Secret Keeper

Relief washed over the boys. They were alive and they'd escaped with their treasures. However, the relief didn't last long, as the adrenaline faded, the silence pressed in. Panic quickly overtook its place.

They were trapped.

The cavern was pitch dark. No shimmering walls, no guiding glow from the minerals, just the narrow cones of light from their headlamps. Dust hung in the air, thick and unmoving.

Smarty Pants sat on the floor, feeling his ankle pulse in throbbing pain. He took a few deep breaths to try and push his pain away, he knew his ankle would have to wait until he escaped the mine. As he moved to stand, his hands sank into the wet, muddy earth. Drops of water were sprinkling all around. When he stood, he winced from the weight being placed on his ankle, but then he turned to help his friend up. As he pulled Fraidy to standing, he noticed the small folded piece of paper nestled in the tight grip of Fraidy Cat's hand.

"What's that?" Smarty Pants asked, nodding toward Fraidy Cat's clenched fist.

Fraidy Cat blinked, startled. "Oh." He slowly opened his hand, revealing a crumpled piece of yellowed paper. "It was under the diamond. I grabbed it without thinking. I don't even know what it is or if it is even important."

Smarty Pants grinned. "You saved a clue. Maybe you're a better detective than you think."

Fraidy Cat smiled proudly. He knew that he sometimes did brave things out of necessity, but this was different. In that moment, back in the glowing chamber, he had a gut feeling that called to him, beckoning him to grab the paper, even if it meant risking safety.

He began to unfold the paper, chest more puffed up than usual. When the paper was completely exposed, they angled their headlamps together, the twin beams lighting up the faded handwriting.

If you are reading this, you are now responsible for the safety of the Mother Diamond. She was not safe in the museum, not with the attempt to steal her. The Bawden family believes they are her rightful owners, but they are wrong. Her beauty cannot be owned or sold. She is a gift of the earth. A gift for the earth.

I, Elias Carver, took the diamond from the museum and returned

Her home. Before I leave this earth, I will pass this knowledge to my brother, Edwin, and him to whom he chooses before his passing. Until then, I remain the Secret Keeper.

But now, since you are reading this, the torch has passed to you. When it is safe, share her beauty again with the town. Until then, keep her hidden. Do not lose her. Protect her at all costs.

Elias Carver

"The Secret Keeper?" Fraidy Cat repeated, his voice barely above a whisper.

Smarty Pants' mind was already racing. "That explains everything. Elias must've written this after he took the diamond. Remember the first note at the museum, the one about the 'true owners'? That had to come from the Bawden family because they were planning on stealing the diamond because they thought it was owed to them. But the note from when the diamond was stolen and this one... they're from Elias himself."

Fraidy Cat shook his head, not hearing what Smarty Pants was saying. "I don't want to be the Secret Keeper. Edwin went mad after learning this. Remember his journal? The responsibility of keeping the Mother Diamond safe *consumed* him."

Smarty Pants' jaw tightened with concern. They both saw the journal and it was terrifying how mad Edwin went. The secret of the Mother Diamond consumed him until his death. "That's not going to happen to you. We're returning the Mother Diamond to the museum where she belongs. She shouldn't be hidden anymore."

A small amount of relief passed through Fraidy Cat. If they shared the Mother Diamond with the world again, if she could be kept safe, then there would be no need for a secret keeper anymore. He would be freed from the curse.

Smarty Pants looked down at the Mother Diamond resting in his hands. It was heavier than it looked, the weight of history pressing into his palms. Its cool surface soothed the cuts and bruises on his skin. For a moment, it almost felt... alive.

Smarty blinked hard, shaking off the thought. A part of him was hoping that the power of the Mother Diamond would heal his ankle, however, he didn't believe in legends. But still, something about the stone felt different.

Smarty Pants gently wrapped the Mother Diamond in his spare jacket he brought and gently placed it inside his backpack.

"Uh... Smarty?" Fraidy Cat said softly. "How are we supposed to get out of here?"

Looking around, the boys surveyed their new location. Puddles littered the floor from drippings above. No mine cart tracks were present to lead them down the yellow brick road. They were completely alone in unfamiliar territory with no promise of escape.

Smarty returned to the moment. In all the excitement, he'd forgotten the most obvious problem: they were trapped. "Right," he said. "We can't go back the way we came. Let's follow the tunnel. Maybe it connects to another exit."

Hesitant to wander down a tunnel with no promise of seeing the sun again, Fraidy Cat followed his friend. He knew that if he stayed there, he would certainly remain trapped forever. However, if he followed Smarty Pants, there was a possibility of escaping.

As they headed down the tunnel, it turned a corner, opening into a narrow passageway that gaped in the rock. The wooden beams lining the walls told them it was part of the old mine network, yet the exact location remained unknown.

They walked for what felt like hours. The tunnel sloped downward, then twisted again. Nothing looked familiar, no trace of the mine tracks, gate, or forked path they had once passed. This was a new vein in the mine system. Fraidy Cat couldn't shake the feeling that they were heading deeper into the earth; digging their own grave with every step.

Then, a whisper of cool, fresh air brushed against Smarty's sweaty forehead. He halted, stunned with hope.

"Wind," he said. "That means... outside."

Without waiting, he started to run, or at least his version of running with his injured ankle. He was praying that this was the exit he was dreaming of. Fraidy Cat followed close behind, his breath echoing in the narrow tunnel. The air grew cooler, fresher. The dirt under their boots began to change, softer, mixed with pine needles.

Then, all at once, the darkness broke.

Trees surrounded them. The night sky opened above, the moon lighting the scenery. And for the first time in hours, they could breathe.

They stumbled out of the mine, collapsing onto the cold ground, gulping air like it was treasure. But when they finally looked around, they realized this wasn't the entrance they'd used. They had no idea where they were.

Smarty Pants dug into his backpack and pulled out his compass. The needle pointed north, home. They followed it through the trees until the familiar outline of the main mine entrance came into view.

Covered in dirt, exhausted but grinning, they bent over, catching their breath, officially feeling like they escaped. They quickly freed their scooters, thankful that the chain kept them safe, and started down the hillside. The wind rushed through their mud ridden hair, and above them, the stars shimmered like scattered diamonds.

However, the largest diamond of all was in Smarty Pants' backpack; the reason for Fraidy Cat's mom disappearing.

They had found the Mother Diamond.

Now, they had to find Fraidy Cat's mom.

16

The Message in the Window

Out of breath, the boys finally made it to the safety of Fraidy Cat's neighborhood. Once surrounded by endless trees, they were now passing familiar houses. The smooth road was a much needed relief compared to the bumpy terrain they had been on.

As Fraidy Cat's house came into view, the boys sped up, eager to lay in their beds. Suddenly, before he reached the safety of his home, Fraidy Cat stopped dead in his tracks in front of one house in particular: Mr. Kadburgler's. His gut twisted. The secrets to this mystery–the diamond, his mother missing– lived inside that house.

Mr. Kadburgler was the grandson of Henry Bawden, the man who once claimed to be the rightful owner of the Mother Diamond. The one who threatened to steal the Mother Diamond from the museum, willing to do anything to have the diamond for himself.

The apple probably didn't fall far from the tree. Fraidy Cat just *knew* Mr. Kadburgler had to be involved with his mother's disappearance.

Smarty Pants stopped beside his friend. Together, they stared, trying to make sense of the secrets behind those drawn curtains. A silhouette flickered across a curtain in the upstairs hall window, freezing them in place. But after a few moments of nothing, the boys finally turned away and trudged home.

They abandoned their scooters at the front door, collapsed inside, and spent the next hour eating whatever they could find and rinsing off the layers of mine dust still clinging to their skin. Smarty Pants did his best at wrapping his bruised purple ankle, but knew that it wasn't going to fix anything. He kept the extent of his injury to himself, not wanting to give Fraidy Cat another thing to worry about.

Freshly showered and dressed, they crawled into their beds, their one safe place, and let their thoughts replay the day like a movie.

When sleep finally took hold, so did their dreams.

Smarty Pants dreamt of the Mother Diamond; of being celebrated as the boy who returned it to the world.

Fraidy Cat dreamt of something far more special: his mother's smiling face.

The night passed quietly for once. No bumps, no shattering glass, just peace. When morning light filled the room, the boys kept sleeping, worn out from their adventure.

It wasn't until nearly noon that Smarty Pants blinked awake. The sunlight glinting through the window looked just like the glow of the Mother Diamond.

The Mother Diamond.

Heart racing, he leapt from his makeshift bed and started digging through Fraidy Cat's closet.

Fraidy Cat jolted up, startled by the noise and the random articles of clothing that were being thrown about his room. Smarty Pants let out a sigh of relief, holding up the diamond he'd hidden the night before.

With the diamond secured, the boys moved like zombies, dragging themselves to breakfast, eating in silence. As they shoveled cereal into their mouths, their minds were blank, exhausted from solving Edwin's riddle.

Then—*scrape.*

A sharp, repetitive sound cut through the morning calm.

The boys exchanged glances, waking their brains and bringing them back to the mystery at hand. Smarty Pants remembered that he was still on the case and Fraidy Cat remembered his mom was still missing.

They crept to the nearest window, Smarty Pants still limping from his ankle, but doing his best to look normal. When they got to the window, the image they saw made the hairs on their necks stand straight up. Outside, in the yard next to Fraidy's, Mr. Kadburgler was shoveling something out of the dirt in his backyard.

Fraidy Cat's mind raced. *What could he be digging up? Or worse yet, what could he be burying? Was his mom…?*

Before he could finish the thought he dreaded, both boys moved upstairs for a better view. From the second-story window, they could see clearly now: sweat beading on Mr. Kadburgler's forehead, yellow leather gloves gripping the shovel, a large, empty hole hopefully still too shallow for whatever it was meant to hold.

Fraidy Cat clutched the windowsill, weak, steadying himself. The hole was *just long enough* for an adult body.

Breath faltering, Fraidy Cat went numb. Realizing the thought process that was cycling through Fraidy's brain, Smarty Pants leaned into his friend, nudging him with his shoulder. This small brush of physical contact reminded Fraidy that he needed to keep fighting for answers. He couldn't break now.

"She's fine," Smarty Pants said softly, turning to rest a hand on his friend's shoulder.

"How do you know? What if we are working so hard for nothing? What if we are already too late?" Fraidy closed his eyes as he thought of these questions, afraid of their answers.

"I just know. My gut says to keep going and everything will work out. We can't give up now."

"But Mr. Kadburgler is digging a hole! What can we do to stop him now?" Desperation sinking deeper into Fraidy's shoulders.

"We'll keep an eye on him. Make sure nothing goes in that hole. And tonight, we go in, and find out what he's hiding."

"*In?* As in *inside* his house?" Fraidy Cat gasped. If this was Smarty Pants' idea of comfort, he wanted none of it. "No way! I already went inside a mine and nearly died. I am *not* going into that creep's house!"

"But what if your mom is in there?" Smarty Pants reminded his friend of what was at stake.

Fraidy Cat swallowed hard. He'd always said he'd do *anything* for his mom. Apparently, that included facing all of his fears. Tonight he would be walking straight into the belly of the beast.

"Fine," he muttered reluctantly.

"Let's stake his place out for a bit," Smarty Pants said. "We'll need to know what we're walking into."

They marked every window in the house that gave a view of Mr. Kadburgler's property and began rotating shifts, tracking his every move through a pair of old binoculars.

Three hours had passed and all they'd learned was that Mr.

Kadburgler was *boring.* He read the newspaper for an hour, stared at his petunias for another, and occasionally just stared at walls. At this point though, they had been watching the closed bathroom door, Mr. Kadburgler had been in there for almost an hour.

Just as the boys were about to give up, movement caught their attention. In the attic window, there it was again. The shadow.

Only this time, it didn't bang or vanish. It just stood there... watching Fraidy Cat's house.

Fog began to form on the cloudy window in front of the shadow. Then, in one swift motion, it raised a hand and wrote a single word into the glass:

HELP.

17

The Lion's Den

"It's her! I have to go save her!" Fraidy Cat bolted toward the door, his heart pounding faster than his feet could move. The only thing he could think of was finally seeing his mom again, safe, alive, and free.

Smarty Pants darted in front of him, ignoring the searing pain that moved up his leg, spreading his arms wide to block the doorway. "Stop, Fraidy! We have to think smart about this."

"There isn't anything you can say that's going to stop me from going over there right now!" Fraidy's voice cracked.

"You could put her in more danger if you barge in there—and yourself too."

"I guess there is something you can say that will stop me." Fraidy Cat had so many conflicting emotions harbored in his body that he didn't know how to react at this moment. He was still scared, but now he was more scared for his mom than himself. "I don't want her in more danger. I want to save her."

"Then we need a plan," Smarty said, calm but firm. "We can't be reckless. If we rush in, Kadburgler wins."

Fraidy hesitated. He hated that Smarty was right. He didn't want to wait any longer to save his mom, but he knew it was the rational thing to do.

The boys headed to the office to work out their plan, which had to be fool proof.

Their center of operations looked different now. Rather than the journal being open with other papers used for research, they were brainstorming how to get into Mr. Kadburgler's house, papers flying as they scribbled ideas, crossed them out, and argued over what might work. After an hour and a mountain of crumpled paper, they stepped out of the room with tired eyes but a solid plan.

They packed small bags with only the necessities: rope, a flashlight, walkie-talkies, and a few tools to attempt lock picking if needed, but hoping they didn't. They dressed in dark clothes that would blend into the fleshly night sky. Smarty Pants secretly wrapped his ankle again, but the swelling was getting bigger.

Fraidy Cat and Smarty Pants sat at the kitchen table. They went over the plan again and again until they could recite it by heart.

When it was finally time, they stood silently by the back yard sliding glass door. As they prepared to put their plan in motion, they thought back to a few days ago when they stood in that exact spot. Then they were looking for dancing shadows from a cryptic sandwich message, now they were on a rescue mission to free Fraidy's mom. Both boys took one last deep breath knowing the risk they were taking.

The click of the latch unlocking was their point of no return.

Outside, the night swallowed them whole. They moved like shadows across Fraidy Cat's backyard, pressing against the wooden fence, trying to disappear into the dark. Peeking through a crack between the slats, Smarty saw that the coast was clear. There was no sign of Mr. Kadburgler.

They hooked the trampoline ladder over the fence. Smarty went first, scaling the fence and dropping softly into the darkness on the other side, trying to land on his sole good foot. Fraidy followed, landing beside him.

They had now entered enemy territory.

They scanned the yard. No sound, no movement. Not even a whisper of wind. Fraidy's stomach churned when he saw the shallow hole in the dirt, the same one Kadburgler had been digging earlier. At least it was still empty. For now.

They quickly dashed across the perfectly manicured lawn, not wanting to be exposed for longer than necessary. When they reached the back door, Smarty pressed himself against the wall and peered through the window. The kitchen was empty.

Hoping it was unlocked, he tried the door knob and it turned easily.

With the door open, they slowly slipped inside. The air smelled like dust and old coffee. The floorboards groaned under their weight, so they stepped in sync, each foot falling where the others had just left.

Passing through the kitchen, they reached a narrow hallway lined with picture frames. None showed Mr. Kadburgler. Every single one was an image of the past. It started with Maple Hollow Mine in its prime: miners smiling beside carts of ore, sunlight glinting off the rocks.

The shrine of Maple Hollow Mine and the Bawden riches soon faded into its downfall. As the pictures went on, the smiles faded. Prosperity turned to ruin. The last frame wasn't a photograph at all but a newspaper clipping–the same one the boys had found behind the Carver brothers' picture frame in Fraidy Cat's mom's office. Across the article, in angry red ink, was the word:

THIEVES.

Fraidy shivered. The air felt colder here, filled with rage and revenge.

The boys crept out of the hallway into a dark living room. The only light came from the moon slipping through thin curtains. Dust motes floated like ghosts in the air.

When they reached the staircase, both boys waited. A flight of wooden stairs sat before them. Disappointment took hold of them, they knew how creaky wooden stairs could be. Eager to not cause any noise in the house, they took the stairs one at a time.

Smarty went first. Step one, silent. Step two, silent. Step three, still silent. Step four...

CREEEAK.

The sound echoed through the house like a scream. Smarty stiffened mid-step, breath locked in his chest. Slowly, he lifted his foot and lunged over the step, landing on the fifth. Silence again.

Step by careful step, they climbed the rest of the stairs until they had reached the hallway. Then they saw it, at the end of the hallway was an attic ladder already pulled down, inviting them to uncover its secrets.

They exchanged a look. This was it.

One by one, they climbed. Smarty reached the top first, extending a hand to pull Fraidy up.

The attic was dim and dusty, filled with old furniture and boxes. In the middle of it all, tied to a chair and lit by a sliver of moonlight, sat Fraidy's mom.

"Mmph!" she tried to yell through the scarf tied around her mouth, eyes wide with panic.

"Mom!" Fraidy whispered, running forward.

But she shook her head frantically, muffled words trying to warn them.

Creak.

A new sound, heavier, slower, came from behind them.

Fraidy turned.

From the shadows, Mr. Kadburgler stepped into the light, his eyes cold and triumphant.

He'd been waiting for them.

The sinister curl of his mustache lifted into a smile. "Well, well," he said softly. "Welcome to the lion's den."

18

The Deal with the Devil

The boys stumbled backward, trying to distance themselves from Mr. Kadburgler. Fraidy Cat moved so fast he tripped, scrambling backward across the dusty floor trying get back on his feet. Muffled screams emitted from Merilyn, doing all she could to help her son.

With the click of a button from a remote in Mr. Kadburgler's hand, Merilyn quieted in silent pain. Wrapped around her neck was a shock collar. "You like my little toy?" their captor chuckled, flaunting the remote at Fraidy Cat. "It is extremely effective. Wide range. Allows me to stay in control of her even, let's say, when I'm doing yard work and she gets out of control and bangs on the window!" Mr. Kadburgler shot her a spiteful look as he clicked the button again, emitting a shock.

Turning his attention to his new guests, Mr. Kadburgler walked closer to the boys, circling them slowly, every step heavy with menace. Smarty Pants tracked his movements, mind racing for an escape plan. The man continued his circle around the boys, then walked toward his real target, stopping only when he stood behind Fraidy Cat's mom, the large attic window behind him. He set his hands on her shoulders as if to claim her, daring Fraidy Cat to fight him.

Both boys remained still, unsure of what to do in this situation. They'd known getting caught was possible but not like this. Not with him waiting for them. Their plan was to get in and out without him noticing them. But he trapped them. Now he was in total control, their plan useless.

"I'm so glad you could join us," Mr. Kadburgler bellowed, a crooked grin stretching beneath his mustache. "Merilyn and I were getting bored waiting for you to arrive. I saw you watching me and knew my little message to you on the window would send you right over. And we have been waiting for you all day." He squeezed her shoulders as he spoke, she let out a wince in pain.

"That was you?" Smarty Pants exhaled, defeated.

"Let her go!" Fraidy Cat shouted, his voice cracking with fear and fury.

"Why would I do that," Mr. Kadburgler said coolly, "when the fun is just getting started?"

"What do you want from us?" Smarty Pants demanded, his voice steady but cautious.

"You know what I want." Kadburgler's eyes glinted. "I've seen you piecing it all together. I've followed you! I want what's mine! What's owed to me!" Spit was flying out of his mouth with every word.

A chill crept up the boys' spines. They had just found the Mother Diamond and now they were about to lose it.

"We don't have it with us," Smarty Pants said, locking eyes with the man who had been plaguing his nightmares, unwilling to show weakness.

"I've waited this long for my family's treasure to be returned," Kadburgler hissed. "I can wait for you to fetch it and deliver it to me." His grip was still tight on Merilyn.

"Please," Fraidy Cat begged, "just let her go! We'll bring it right back!"

Kadburgler laughed; a sound that deafened the air and rattled the dusty boxes in the attic. It wasn't human. It was hollow and sharp, like nails on glass. Merilyn's eyes were pleading to Fraidy Cat to just leave her there and save himself.

"Let her go?" he mocked. "She's the only reason you'll do as I say. Bring me the diamond, and then..." He paused, the corners of his mouth twitching upward. "... I'll let you all go."

The look in his eyes told them the truth, he had no intention of letting anyone go.

A muffled gasp escaped Merilyn's gag as Kadburgler's fingers dug deeper into her shoulder.

"Okay!" Fraidy Cat blurted out. "We'll get it! Just don't hurt her anymore! We will bring you the diamond, just get your filthy hands off of her."

"I'm not done playing with her yet. Bring me a new toy—a shiny one—and then you can have her." He pointed a bony finger at Fraidy. "You'll bring my diamond to me." His gaze slid toward Smarty Pants with disdain, daring him to stand up to him now.

"But I can't leave her..." Fraidy's voice shook.

"Let's go, Fraidy," Smarty Pants interrupted, realizing there was no rationalizing with this mad man, he grabbed his friend by the shirt. Fraidy Cat resisted, unable to leave his mother, but Smarty Pants overpowered him. He dragged him toward the opening in the floor, forcing him down the ladder before he could argue. It was the only way to get him out safely.

"I know you know your way back in!" Kadburgler's voice echoed behind them. "Be quick or I'll have to do something drastic!" Another gasp of pain from Merilyn echoed through the house.

This threat motivated the boys. They tore through the house; down the creaky stairs, past the dusty curtains and crooked frames, through the back door, across the lawn, up the ladder, until finally, they burst into Fraidy's kitchen.

"My mom! What are we going to do?" Fraidy gasped, clutching the counter for balance. "We left her with that monster!"

Smarty Pants suddenly collapsed to the floor, no longer able to tolerate the pain of his ankle. Fraidy Cat quickly moved to his friend, not wanting to see someone else he loved be in pain again. "What's wrong?"

Smarty Pants lifted his pant leg, removed his shoe, and un-wrapped his ankle, revealing his purple, swollen injury. "I think I'm hurt. Like really hurt." His voice sounded more scared than he would have liked to admit.

"Why didn't you tell me?" Concern draped across Fraidy Cat's face.

"You already had too much to worry about." Smarty Pants gave an awkward chuckle, he didn't like to admit he had weaknesses. "Besides, it's going to be fine. I just need to use it for a little bit longer. Just until we get your mom back."

"No! You can't go back over there on this. You need to rest." Fraidy Cat knew what this meant and shivered at the thought. "I'll go alone..."

"I won't let you!"

"Look at your ankle! If you come, I'll just have to worry about you too, and I can't save my mom if I'm doing that." Fraidy Cat didn't know if he was trying to convince Smarty Pants or himself of accepting this new plan. "We are running out of time. This is how it has to be."

"Fine. But I'm going to help you from here then."

Looking at the clock on the microwave, one minute had passed. They hurried upstairs, Fraidy Cat supporting his friend like a human crutch. Smarty Pants set up his look out spot by the window with binoculars in one hand and a walkie-talkie in the other, ankle propped up on a pillow stacked on a chair. If he couldn't go with Fraidy, he would still keep watch, listening in, protecting him from afar.

Fraidy Cat turned to leave Smarty Pants alone in the room, knowing he would be making the rest of this journey alone, trying to abandon his fears. As Fraidy reached the doorway, Smarty Pants called out to him.

"I have an idea," Smarty said. "We're not just going to save your mom. We're going to save the Mother Diamond too."

19

The Keeper's Secret

Fraidy Cat walked the familiar path back to Mr. Kadburgler's house alone. No Smarty Pants by his side, no comfort or plan to cling to, only the thought of his mother's safety driving him forward. He grasped the trampoline ladder that was hanging on the fence, feet safely planted in his own backyard. Inhaling, he prepared for battle, knowing he would not be leaving that house without his mom.

As he climbed the rungs, he replayed the conversations that tormented him; those that told him he wasn't good enough, smart enough, brave enough. The echoes of kids chanting "Fraidy Cat" around him while he curled up in a ball. Balancing on the top of the fence, he began to falter under his self doubt. Catching himself, he could hear Smarty Pants in his mind, standing up for him; defending him. He remembered all that he had accomplished over these last few days; braving a mine, digging up treasure in his backyard, confronting Mr. Kadburgler. He was brave. He is brave. Closing his eyes, he exhaled his self doubt, removing it from his body. As he opened his eyes, brave and confident, he jumped.

As he crossed the dark lawn, the weight of the diamond in his jacket pocket pulled at him every step, bringing him closer to Mr. Kadburgler's house; closer to saving his mom. But heavier still was the ache in his chest hoping he wouldn't lose everything during this exchange.

He stepped through Mr. Kadburgler's back door. As he passed through the narrow hallway, the portraits of the Bawden lineage glared down from their dusty frames. Their painted eyes seemed to follow him, taunting him. Victory plastered on their faces, certain the diamond would be theirs soon.

He reached the stairs, dust drifting up his nose, his legs heavy. Climbing the stairs this time, he welcomed the screeches, he wanted Mr. Kadburgler to know he was coming for him. He wanted him to feel some of the fear he had been causing. At the base of the attic ladder, he stopped. Above him was danger. Above him was his mother. Above him was the moment that would decide everything. Finally, he felt prepared for it.

He took a shaky breath and thought of Smarty Pants and of his steady voice, his quick plans, his courage. Then he reached out and gripped the first rung. "I can do this," he whispered. "I *am* brave."

The moonlight from the attic spilled down the opening. When Fraidy climbed through, Mr. Kadburgler was waiting, still gripping his mother's shoulders. His face gleamed with greedy excitement.

"Where is your little friend?" Mr. Kadburgler snarled through his teeth.

"He got hurt." Fraidy Cat's voice cracked. He took a gulp and steadied himself. "I brought what you wanted."

"I'll have to deal with him later," Mr. Kadburgler mumbled under his breath. "Well," he said, his voice thick with satisfaction, "where is it?"

"I have it," Fraidy said, resting his hand over the lump in his jacket. "But first, I want to know why? Why do all this? Why take my mom? We didn't even know anything about your stupid family legacy or the Mother Diamond!"

"Why?" Kadburgler barked, anger flashing in his eyes. "Because your family *ruined* mine! That diamond was rightfully ours. It could have restored our fortune but your family stole it. They hid it until the mine was closed and went back for it, claiming it was theirs!"

"That's not true!" Fraidy snapped. "They went back *after* the mine shut down to get their tools! That's when they *found* the Mother Diamond. Your family already had lost everything."

"That is the story Elias and Edwin told, but they are liars" Kadburgler sneered. "They were nobodies! Dirt under my great-grandfather's boots! They had *no right* to take that gem!"

"Your grandfather, Henry Bawden, was a gambler and a cheat!" Fraidy shot back. "He destroyed his own legacy!"

Kadburgler's face twisted with rage. With a furious roar, he lunged at Fraidy Cat. However, Fraidy dodged, and they ended up on opposite sides of the attic's door in the floor; Merilyn remained tied to the chair by the window, shoulders now free from her captor's piercing nails.

The man steadied himself, eyes narrowing. "Your mother was useless," he said coldly. "She only knew the legend behind the Mother Diamond, nothing about where Elias and Edwin hid it, or so she pretended." He glanced at Merilyn, smirking. "So I had to step in. A little fear tends to make people talk. A few well-timed threatening letters did the trick. The ones where I threatened you, that really got to her." Mr. Kadburgler spat in her direction, hatred fueling him. "She wasn't giving me the information I needed though!"

Merilyn shook with anger, trying to release herself from the binds that held her to the chair.

"I had to get her alone. I needed to force her to talk. So I played her. I knew she would help her poor, old neighbor carry in some groceries. She walked right into my house. So I guess you can say I didn't take her, she came here willingly" a gross and sadistic smile growing on his face.

Fraidy clenched his fists.

"But then," Kadburgler continued, "you and your little genius friend started poking around. Stealing your bikes, breaking into your house, following you; it was all *so easy* to nudge you along, letting you do all the hard work for me. You found my diamond.

And now you're going to hand it over."

Fraidy swallowed hard. He'd heard enough. "So that's it? You admit it?"

Kadburgler's grin faltered. "What? Were you not paying attention?"

"You *admit* you sent the letters. You kept her hostage. You stole our bikes. You broke into my house. You did everything! You..."

Before he could finish, Kadburgler lunged again, determined to retrieve the diamond Fraidy Cat hid in his pocket. Gripping the object hidden within the jacket, Kadburgler yanked it, freeing it from its hiding place. "Give me my diamond!" he roared, shoving Fraidy backward into his mother's lap.

But when Kadburgler looked down, triumph quickly faded from his face, replacing it with confusion. In his hand was not a gem but a walkie-talkie, its button held down by a rubber band, red light glowing.

"Thank you for that confession," Fraidy said, breathless but smiling. "The police are going to love hearing it."

Across the street, Smarty Pants held the second walkie-talkie, recorder pressed against it, capturing every word; the police had already been called and were on their way.

Mr. Kadburgler began fumbling, he was losing control of the situation. His face turned red with fury. "You think that'll stop me? By the time the police come, I'll be long gone! Now where is my DIAMOND!"

The entire house seemed to quake at his roar.

Fraidy reached into his other pocket. The diamond glimmered in his hand, the faint moonlight illuminating it. "You want it? *Go get it!*"

He hurled it down the attic opening. A sharp crash echoed through the house as the gem shattered into glittering fragments.

"No!" Kadburgler howled. He dove after it, disappearing into the darkness below.

Without hesitation, Fraidy yanked the ladder up and slammed the attic door shut. He dragged every heavy box and crate he could find, piling them on top until the door was buried.

Then he ran to his mother. Her wrists were raw, her face pale, but she was alive. He untied the knots with shaking hands, removed the collar that was clipped around her neck, and tore off the scarf covering her mouth before wrapping his arms around her.

For a moment, neither of them spoke.

When they pulled apart, her eyes were wet with pride.

"We have to get out of here," Fraidy said. "He's still down there."

"There's no other door," she warned.

Fraidy turned toward the window, the same one that once haunted his dreams. "There is now."

He threw the chair his mother once sat in through the window, cool night air rushing in through the shattered glass. Across the way, Smarty Pants leaned out Fraidy's window, walkie-talkie in hand, a grin spreading across his face.

They'd done it.

Then...

BANG!

The attic floor shook. Kadburgler pounded from below.

Fraidy met his mother's eyes. "We have to jump."

20

The Leap to Freedom

They climbed out the window, balancing on the edge of the roof. From the ground, the jump looked easy. But up here, staring down into the darkness, it felt like a drop straight to their doom.

Fraidy Cat's courage began to waver, every ounce of bravery already spent in the fight above. He took a step back toward the window, the safety of the attic calling him. But a thunderous *bang* from beneath the buried door snapped him to attention.

His mother reached out her hand, eyes locked on his.

"You can do this," she said softly. "Remember, you *are* brave."

"I can't." Fraidy Cat was clutching the wall, silent tears streaming down his face. The rush of emotions shaking his body.

Grabbing his chin, Merilyn met her son's eyes, tears developing in her own eyes too. "Look at what you have already done. You can do this. I know you can."

Fraidy took her hand. A surge of strength filled him. Together, they edged closer to the ledge, climbing down the tapered roof, getting closer to the ground. The cool night air brushed their faces. Another heavy pound rattled the roof from above them.

Before he could over analyze the situation again, they jumped.

The world blurred in a rush of wind and then *thud!* They hit the perfectly trimmed lawn, rolling onto their backs. For a moment, they just lay there, breathing, alive, and feeling the aches and pains from their drop, but free from the walls that had held them prisoner.

Then came the wail of sirens.

Red and blue lights flashed through the quiet neighborhood, bouncing off windows and trees. Neighbors had begun opening their doors, peering over at the commotion.

Fraidy pushed himself up only to be tackled to the ground again. He gasped then laughed when he saw the familiar face grinning down at him.

"Smarty Pants! You're supposed to be resting your ankle!"

"But we did it! You did it!" His best friend had hobbled down the stairs and out on the front yard, adrenaline ignoring any pain his ankle brought. He hugged him tight, proud of him for executing their plan perfectly.

They had done it.

Every sleepless night, every fear, every dark tunnel and clue, it had all led here. His mom was safe. They had solved the mystery.

Their moment of triumph didn't last long. Police officers approached them, hurrying them off the lawn and toward the patrol cars. From behind the blinking lights, they saw officers pouring into Mr. Kadburgler's house.

As they emerged from the house, Mr. Kadburgler had his arms cuffed behind him, sweat dripping off his wrinkled forehead. While the officers led him across his yard, he kept muttering to himself, "I was so close. It was mine. What has he done?" Fraidy Cat and Smarty Pants chuckled at the sight. They couldn't believe that was the man they were scared of, he looked pathetic. Merilyn just glared, defiant. For a brief moment, Mr. Kadburgler had met her eyes, causing him to scream in her direction, the officers responded by quickly placing him in a squad car.

"Karma," Merilyn murmured as they slammed the door on him, rubbing the red marks still lining her wrists.

Back at Fraidy Cat's house, the chaos settled into calm.

Smarty Pants' parents arrived, rushing to hug their son. With Smarty Pants' ankle properly looked at by the paramedics and both the families reunited in the Carver's kitchen, the police officers asked questions for hours, piecing together the story until there was nothing left to tell. Fraidy Cat and Smarty Pants even had a few questions themselves.

"I was getting threatening letters for a couple weeks." Merilyn was explaining to the police officers what had happened before she got kidnapped. "They kept getting worse and worse. They wanted the Mother Diamond. I didn't really know anything about it. My late husband told me stories of the legend of it and how his great grandpa discovered it." Merilyn took a drink of water, her throat sore from being trapped the last few days. "Before my husband passed, he gave me a key and told me to keep it safe. He mentioned something about being a Secret Keeper?"

Fraidy Cat and Smarty Pants looked at each other. They couldn't believe that Fraidy Cat's dad knew about the diamond.

"I finally got a note telling me to meet at the old church or they would hurt Freddy. I was really scared, scared of Freddy getting hurt, but also of leaving Freddy alone. I left him the hidden notes before I left as a fail safe. Just in case I didn't return. If I did return, he wouldn't have found them and then he would stay safe. But if things went wrong, he would know I didn't just leave him. I would never abandon him. I was on my way out to the old church when Mr. Kadburgler asked me if I could help him bring in some groceries. I occasionally helped him and I didn't think it would take too much time, but when I got inside his house, he attacked me and locked me up in the attic. I watched from the foggy attic window as the silhouette of my car was moved into his garage." The police nodded as they wrote down her story.

"Was it you?" Fraidy Cat looked up at his mom, hoping to finally receive an answer.

"Was what me?" she responded with a curious chuckle.

"The phone call that first night. Warning us to not trust anyone, was that you?" Fraidy Cat was now looking down, preparing to hear the wrong answer.

Merilyn eyed her son up and down, heart aching at the sight of his pain. "Yes", she whispered, placing her arm around him. "I was constantly trying to escape, to return to you. When he first trapped me, he left me untied up there." She shivered, remembering her prison. "I found an old phone up there, honestly I was surprised it even worked. When I saw him head over to the house, I had to warn you about him, but before I could, he came back." She hung her head, disappointed in herself for not getting enough communicated to them on that fateful night.

"You did." Fraidy was now comforting his mom. "You led us in the right direction that night. We would have never found the diamond if you didn't call us and leave those notes pointing us to Edwin and Elias."

"Yeah, Mrs. C. You were the reason we were able to find everything and rescue you!" Smarty Pants chimed in.

The boys recounted their story to the police officers. They described their trip into the mine, however, they altered their story a little bit to make it sound safer when they saw the worry on their parents' faces, cutting out many parts of their adventure.

Eventually, the flashing lights of the cop cars faded, leaving the neighborhood wrapped once more in sleepy silence.

The house, once empty and cold, now pulsed with warmth. Merilyn, too shaken to be alone, asked the Shelleys to stay the night in the guest room.

When the boys finally crawled into their beds, Smarty Pants was out like a light, his dreams full of cheers and victory. Fraidy Cat, though, couldn't sleep. Every creak of the house made his eyes snap open, half-expecting Mr. Kadburgler's shadow to appear once more.

At last, unable to bear it, he slipped from his bed and crept to his mother's room. She sat upright in bed, just as restless. When she saw him, she smiled wearily and patted the spot beside her on the bed.

Fraidy climbed in, curling close.

"Mom, what do you know about the key you left me in the box? Dad's old key?" Fraidy finally let the question slip that had been replaying in his mind, alluding to the tin box she buried.

"It was my job to keep it safe." Curious, he sat up right, staring at his mom, hoping for the full truth to finally be revealed. "Before dad's accident, he told me bits and pieces of the legend of the Mother Diamond. Honestly, I think he told me everything he knew about it, it just wasn't a lot. Then one day he slipped the key off from around his neck and placed it around mine. He told me I had to keep it safe; be the Secret Keeper. He told me to pass it on to you when you were older."

His face scrunched in confusion, then finally he understood. "So you are the Secret Keeper?" Fraidy Cat questioned with enthusiasm.

Tussling his curly hair, she gave him a wink. "Not anymore. That role was passed down to you. Honestly, I thought it was all a family myth, I didn't even know enough information to know what the secret was, but Mr. Kadburgler started to ask me questions about the Carver history. It intrigued me so I began looking too, however, I didn't really find anything. Just that news article. I never expected a real diamond to be at the end of it though." She smiled, visions of the giant Mother Diamond dancing in her mind. "But the diamond is gone. And that's fine. I got something more valuable here." She gave Fraidy a side shoulder hug, resting their foreheads together. After their embrace, she laid her head down on her pillow, trying to rest after the events from the last few days.

Fraidy Cat laid next to her, relieved he wasn't going to go mad like Edwin.

For the first time in what felt like forever, they both let themselves rest.

And as they drifted into sleep, they knew one thing for certain, their family was whole again.

21

The Last Secret

The smell of pancakes woke Smarty Pants from a deep, dream-less sleep. His nose twitched, following the buttery scent down the hall until he reached the kitchen. There, he stopped and smiled. His parents were sitting at the table laughing, while Merilyn and Fraidy Cat flipped pancakes on the griddle. It was the most comforting sight he'd seen in days.

Taking a seat next to his parents at the round table, he couldn't help but think back on when he had sat there a few days ago with his friend. When he had pried the cling film from the sandwich, unearthing the start of their mystery. Now as he sat at the table, he sat a bit taller, proud of his accomplishments.

When the pancake flipping had ceased, Merilyn placed a large stack on each plate at the table, before taking her own seat. With everyone finally seated, the sound of forks clattering against plates and the smell of maple syrup filled the air. The boys cleared their plates in record time, scrambling to get seconds. Their parents laughed, amazed by how quickly the food disappeared.

"What? We've been living off potato chips for the last few days," Fraidy Cat admitted, his cheeks turning pink. His mom gave him a disapproving look about his food choices knowing there were healthier options stocked in the fridge. "Oh yeah! I did eat a banana", he exclaimed proudly, his mom giving him a subtle smile.

For the remainder of breakfast, the kitchen was filled with laughter and warmth as both families enjoyed being together again.

After breakfast, they gathered in the living room, full and content. The silence that followed was the good kind, the kind that only comes after everything has finally gone right.

Merilyn let out a light laugh. "All that searching, and the Mother Diamond ends up shattered on the floor." The irony of it made her shake her head.

The boys exchanged a glance. That glance said everything.

Their parents immediately picked up on it. "What?" Andrew asked, narrowing his eyes. "What are you two hiding now? I thought we said no more secrets."

"Well…" Smarty Pants began, grinning, "we kind of have one more we haven't told anyone about yet. We just had to wait until we knew it was really safe"

Before anyone could ask, the boys darted out of the room, Smarty Pants still limping. The cozy calm was replaced by puzzled curiosity. Moments later, they returned carrying a small bundle wrapped in cloth.

Fraidy started talking as though giving a presentation, feeling more comfortable in front of others. "You see, I was the Secret Keeper. I am the Secret Keeper. It was my job to keep her safe." Standing proudly before their families, Smarty Pants slowly unfolded his treasure.

As he peeled off the layers of fabric, the room became more illuminated with each reveal. When the fabric was completely removed, exposing its secret, the room lit up in a dazzling display of color as sunlight hit the gem inside.

"The Mother Diamond..." Merilyn whispered, eyes wide.

Stunned shock fluttered through the room, bewildered at the survival of the Mother Diamond.

"I thought you threw it down the stairs to distract your neighbor," Smarty Pants' mom, Ashley, questioned, still confused.

"That's what we wanted him to think," Fraidy Cat replied, smirking.

"Well how did you do it?" Andrew was enthralled with his cunning son.

"It was Mr. Kadburgler's fault," Smarty Pants beamed. "If he hadn't snuck in and smashed the glass bowl, we never would have thought of making a fake. We wouldn't have had the pieces we needed to make it look real."

A proud smile had formed on Ashley's face. "How did you make the glass look like a diamond?" Her voice was squealing with excitement. Her clever son never ceased to amaze her.

Beaming at each other, the boys smirked. "It didn't have to be perfect, just good enough to pass as the Mother Diamond in the dark." Smarty Pants was really pleased with himself.

The night Fraidy Cat had tried to make the trade, the diamond for his mom, Smarty Pants told him of their new plan, the plan to save Merilyn and the Mother Diamond. They quickly pieced together the shattered fragments that were piled on the floor in the corner. A mixture of super glue and hot glue holding the shards together. Stepping back, the boys smiled, it was a decent fake, just good enough to fool Mr. Kadburgler in the dim moonlight.

"And it worked," Fraidy Cat said proudly, returning to the moment of reveal. "We saved you, and the Mother Diamond."

Merilyn sat silent, tears filling her eyes. So many emotions were racing through her body. She couldn't contain her emotions any longer and started crying. Fraidy quickly found his place next to her on the couch, hugging her.

"Are you ok?" Fraidy Cat was investigating her wounds, ankles, wrists, neck, wondering which one was hurting her.

She weakly smiled at him, exhausted from crying. "I'm fine. I'm just proud of you. I'm thankful you are safe. You amaze me. Your father would be proud of you." Tears continued to stream down her face.

Fraidy hugged her tighter. Grateful for the moment.

Smarty Pants moved to sit in between his parents, feeling a bit emotional too. Placing an arm around each of his shoulders, Ashley and Andrew pulled him in for a family hug.

Pulling away, Ashley was blinded by a stray beam of diamond light. Her voice trembled as she asked, "So... what happens now?"

The boys took a moment, pondering all the money they could get from the diamond. Then they thought of all the work they went through to get her, to keep her safe. The generations of people that sacrificed for her in hopes that one day she would be returned to the world. They gave each other a knowing look. There was only one solution.

"We're going to share her with the town again," the boys said in unison, breaking into laughter.

22

The Red Eye

Life settled down for the two families. With Mr. Kadburgler safely behind bars at the state prison, Fraidy Cat and Smarty Pants, ankle now healed, spent the rest of their summer bonding and relaxing in the sun. However, these moments of relaxation were frequently interrupted by phone calls from the Pine City Museum. With the decision to share the Mother Diamond again with the community, the boys had been completely engrossed with her exhibit and safety measures.

When the grand reopening of the Mother Diamond exhibit came around, it drew in record crowds to the Pine City Museum. The story of two boys uncovering a local legend spread far and wide, making them heroes in the eyes of their community, their faces plastered all over the local newspaper.

The Mother Diamond now rested for all to see on a bed of purple velvet, protected by thick layers of glass. A rope surrounded the case with sensors detecting movement, adding a small extra layer of security. Patrons shuffled through the exhibit, children eyeing the diamond with mystery, adults eyeing it with envy.

Smarty Pants and Fraidy Cat stood quietly at the back of the exhibit hall, watching the diamond glitter beneath the lights, relishing in their achievement. They had solved the mystery. They had done what no one else could.

And yet, as the gem sparkled behind its glass case, they both felt something tug at them, a faint restlessness.

With the grand opening over, the boys made no notion of abandoning their post. For days they kept watch over the exhibit, making sure no one tried to steal her again. But when nothing happened, that old feeling returned: the longing for mystery.

"I don't think we need to keep guarding her anymore," Fraidy Cat relented at last. "I guess our Secret Keeper days can retire."

Smarty Pants smiled faintly. "I wonder what Elias and Edwin would say if they were here."

They fell into a thoughtful silence picturing the original Secret Keepers fondly.

"I kind of miss it," Fraidy Cat admitted, fidgeting with his fingers.

"The diamond?" Smarty Pants teased. "It's right there. You can come see it whenever you want. Lifetime memberships, remember?"

Fraidy Cat gave his friend a courteous smile, sighed, and then confessed, "No, the mystery. Solving the puzzles. Being on a case." He looked up, nervous for his friend's response.

However, Smarty Pants nodded, shrugging his shoulders. "Yeah. Me too."

They spent a few more moments, staring at the Mother Diamond, replaying fond memories. Investigating journals, research at the library, finding hidden clues, solving riddles, exploring abandoned mines. It all felt surreal. Remnants of a dream. One, they didn't want to admit, they sometimes wished to revisit.

As they left the exhibit, the boys felt both pride and a hint of sadness. Their adventure was over. They were left longing for a new one.

Weeks passed. Summer ended. School began again.

The boys returned to their normal life after becoming local celebrities. Roaming from class to class, they occasionally got stopped in the hall, with inquiries about their adventure. But for the most part, they faded into the monotony of being students.

As the final bell rang one afternoon, the boys wandered through the hall, chatting about homework, cafeteria food, and their commute home on their brand new bikes. As they reached their lockers, they both began inputting their codes, spinning until they heard the satisfying *click*, their doors swinging open.

Normally, their lockers were kept very tidy, each book having a place, snacks resting on the top shelf. However, to their surprise, a flurry of small papers spilled out of each of their lockers, scattering across the floor.

Fraidy Cat bent down to grab one and froze. Drawn in red ink was the unmistakable image of an eye.

Smarty Pants, holding a small paper he grabbed in midair as it drifted to the floor, a grin spread slowly across his face. As the boys' eyes met, they came to a silent understanding, "Our next mystery."

Note from the Author

Thank you for reading The Mother Diamond. This story began as a set of bedtime tales told to me by my grandfather—stories about two boys, a big mystery, and the courage it takes to follow the truth, even when it feels scary. Writing this book was my way of honoring those stories and sharing them with a new generation of readers.

I hope Fraidy Cat and Smarty Pants reminded you that bravery doesn't mean being fearless, and that curiosity, friendship, and teamwork can lead you to discoveries you never expected to find.

What's Next?

A single symbol changes everything.

In their next mystery, The Curse of the Red Eye, Fraidy Cat and Smarty Pants come face-to-face with a chilling warning—a piece of paper marked with a strange red eye. Those who receive it are said to suffer terrible consequences, and once the symbol appears, there's no turning back.

As rumors spread and danger grows closer, the boys realize this case isn't just about solving a puzzle. It's about survival. With time running out, they must follow the clues, trust each other, and uncover the truth before the curse claims them as its next victims.

Before you go...

Thank you for reading The Mother Diamond. If you enjoyed solving the mystery with Fraidy Cat and Smarty Pants, I'd love to hear what you thought.

Leaving a review on Amazon—whether it's a sentence or two—helps other readers discover the book and lets me know which parts you enjoyed most. Your support means more than you know.

You can also find bonus content, activities, and updates about future mysteries at:

www.ayshajonasbooks.com

I hope you'll join Fraidy Cat and Smarty Pants again soon.

— Aysha Jonas

Acknowledgments

This book would not exist without the love, support, and encouragement of many people.

First, thank you to my family—for believing in this story from the very beginning, for cheering me on during late nights and early mornings, and for reminding me why these stories matter. To my children, thank you for your curiosity, your questions, and your endless imagination. You inspire every page more than you know.

To my grandfather, whose bedtime stories first introduced me to Fraidy Cat and Smarty Pants, thank you for planting the seed that grew into this book. This story is, and always will be, a tribute to you.

Finally, thank you to every reader who picked up this book. Your willingness to follow the clues and search for the truth is what brings this mystery to life.